Nicole couldn't remember the last time her libido was so supercharged.

She was tempted to spend a few more minutes appreciating the handsome picture Daniel made leaning against the wall.

He smiled as she approached. "This is a surprise."

"Weren't you expecting me?" she teased.

"Yeah, just not like this. I was thinking the other day that I couldn't imagine you in jeans."

"Oh, you've been thinking about me?"

Daniel held her gaze. "Yes, ma'am."

A liquid shiver went through her. *Get a grip, Nicole.* How could she facilitate a reconciliation between the Baron children and their mother if she was distracted by the way Daniel Baron filled out a pair of Wranglers?

"So. On a scale from one to I-should-just-throw-myself-from-the-truck, how bad do you think today's gonna be?"

His lips quirked in a half smile. "I don't know," he admitted. "But I'll do what I can to make it as painless as possible."

"You're a really nice guy."

"Actually, I'm more of a cranky loner and recovering troublemaker." His laugh was short and self-deprecating. "Maybe you just bring out my better qualities."

Dear Reader,

If you've read any of my previous books, you probably know I love telling stories about families. So I was excited when the Harlequin editors gave me the flattering challenge of wrapping up the miniseries about the huge Baron family—six siblings in all, each with their own story written by a different author.

The unique opportunity to work with five talented authors made this project extra special. Trish Milburn, author of *The Texan's Cowgirl Bride,* is one of my dearest longtime friends. Now I'm also fortunate to call Donna Alward, Barbara White Daille, Pamela Britton and Cathy McDavid friends. Everyone was enthusiastic and generous, quick to offer brainstorming assistance and encouragement. Building on their stories gave me wonderful supporting characters to work with!

My book tells the story of Daniel Burke Baron, who feels like an outcast among his stepsiblings, so much so that he shies away from the idea of family or ever having kids. Then he meets Nicole Bennett, a woman who's compassionate, gorgeous, determined...and pregnant. I hope you enjoy watching their romance develop and rejoining all the members of the Baron clan for Christmas.

Happy holidays,

Tanya

THE TEXAN'S CHRISTMAS

—

Tanya Michaels

HARLEQUIN® AMERICAN ROMANCE®

Special thanks and acknowledgment are given to Tanya Michaels for her contribution to the Texas Rodeo Barons continuity.

Recycling programs
for this product may
not exist in your area.

ISBN-13: 978-0-373-75543-1

The Texan's Christmas

Copyright © 2014 by Harlequin Books S.A.

Printed in U.S.A.

ABOUT THE AUTHOR

New York Times bestselling author and five-time RITA®
Award nominee Tanya Michaels has been writing love
stories since middle school algebra class (which probably explains her math grades.) Her books, praised for
their poignancy and humor, have received awards from
readers and reviewers alike. Tanya is an active member
of Romance Writers of America and a frequent public
speaker. She lives outside Atlanta with her very supportive husband, two highly imaginative kids and a bichon
frise who thinks she's the center of the universe.

Books by Tanya Michaels

HARLEQUIN AMERICAN ROMANCE

*4 Seasons in Mistletoe
**Hill Country Heroes
***The Colorado Cades

Chapter One

The smell of someone's take-out food filled the crowded elevator, and Nicole Bennett's stomach clenched in protest. *Seafood. Why did it have to be seafood?* Her destination was another five stories up, but when the doors parted at the next floor, she seized her chance to escape. Otherwise, she might make the elevator ride very unpleasant for the other passengers.

Taking deep, cleansing breaths, she headed for the stairwell at the end of the hallway. She'd planned not to tell anyone she was pregnant until after the first trimester, but these attacks of nausea might force her hand. She and Adele had dinner reservations in an hour and a half. How was Nicole going to survive the restaurant if she couldn't stomach food smells?

Every time Nicole thought about sharing her news with Adele Black, she was swamped with conflicting emotions. Her boss had mentored her since Nicole interned at AB Windpower in college. In the past couple of years, when Adele's cancer made it impossible to carry out her normal responsibilities, Nicole had been her second-in-charge. The two women had grown very close—closer than Nicole had been to any of her foster moms during childhood.

There was no one Nicole wanted to share her joy with more, but motherhood was a complicated subject for Adele. Decades ago, after her postpartum depression had spiraled out of control, Adele had abandoned her own four children. When she'd asked later for visitation rights, her powerful ex-husband had said the kids were better off without her and threatened to ruin her if she ever contacted them. Adele had changed her name and built a company, but she'd never had a family again. Would Nicole's news be bittersweet for her?

Then again, since the two women were temporarily sharing the apartment Adele kept near AB Windpower's satellite office in Dallas, maybe hiding the pregnancy wasn't practical.

Trudging up the next set of stairs, Nicole weighed her decision. As vice president of operations, she had a lot of responsibility. The company had lost a few employees this year, and she didn't want to cause her mentor stress about being shorthanded during Nicole's eventual maternity leave. Nicole had hoped to have a couple of new hires in place before she told Adele. Some strong candidates had sent in résumés, but with Christmas right around the corner and holiday plans scheduled, no one wanted to start until after the first of the year.

And can you blame them? What wouldn't she give for family plans? For eager kids insisting it was time to get up and see what Santa had left, for siblings and cousins and grandparents sipping coffee in their flannel pajamas and robes?

She still had one last flight of stairs to go when the cell phone in her suit jacket buzzed. Probably Adele, trying to figure out what was taking so long. But to Nicole's surprise, the name that flashed across her screen was Chris Miller.

Happy holidays, Nic! Any chance you have time to talk this week?

She smiled at the coincidence. Calling her former coworker was actually on her to-do list for tomorrow. Last spring, Chris had been Adele's top choice to run the Dallas office. Life had thrown him some curveballs, though, and in the wake of finding out he was going to be a father, he'd left the company. Maybe his absence was for the best. Nicole didn't know how she would have been able to face him regularly while keeping Adele's secret. Through an odd quirk of fate, the woman Chris had recently married was Adele's oldest daughter.

If this visit to Dallas went the way Nicole hoped, maybe there would no longer be a need for secrecy. She paused on the landing to text him back.

Great minds think alike! Just got to town & was hoping we could all have dinner one night. I'd love to see Lizzie & the baby.

No answer followed. She chalked it up to either his needing to check with Lizzie about details or being interrupted by their newborn. If Nicole didn't get a response tonight, she'd phone him in the morning. In the meantime...

She pulled out her keycard and opened the door to the suite. "Hello? It's me."

Adele moved into view, carrying a bottle and two champagne flutes from the kitchen area into the living room. "About time, dear! I didn't want to celebrate without you."

A grin split Nicole's face. "You got the results?"

Technically, Adele had already been declared cancer-free in San Antonio, but now that she was feeling well enough to travel, she'd wanted a second opinion from a respected specialist in Dallas. It was as if she'd been too afraid to believe she was in remission—as if, perhaps, she didn't believe she deserved it. Adele had done a lot of soul-searching during her illness. At her sickest, she'd frequently spoken about the four children she'd left behind.

Lizzie, Savannah, Carly and Jet had been raised by their father, oil tycoon and rodeo legend Brock Baron. When Adele had feared she might die without getting a chance to tell her grown daughters and son that she was sorry or that she loved them, Nicole had urged her friend to contact them. Adele had balked, insisting she'd caused them enough pain already. It was too cruel to pop back into their lives just to tell them she was dying and to say goodbye. But perhaps now...

"Is that champagne?" Nicole asked, hesitating in the foyer. "I, uh, haven't eaten much today. I'm afraid it might go straight to my head. Wouldn't want to fall asleep on the cab ride to dinner."

Adele shook her head. "Like I'm going to put alcohol into my body on top of everything else? It's just fancy juice. But the exhilaration is real."

Nicole stepped forward to hug her. Despite Adele's fragile frame—she'd lost a ton of weight during treatment—there was strength in the return embrace. *She's improving every day.* Adele's graying hair was short and thin, and she still tended to sport shadows beneath her eyes, but she looked nice tonight. The red tunic sweater she wore added some pink to her cheeks. She was a spot of festive color amid the neutral decor. It gave Nicole an idea.

"You plan to be in Dallas for at least a couple of weeks, right? What if we…what if we get a Christmas tree?" She felt almost shy making the suggestion. Decorating for Christmas was traditionally a family endeavor.

"A tree?" Adele glanced around the room, as if seeking the perfect place to put one. "Yes, I think so. That's a lovely idea. We'll need to buy some ornaments and lights, though."

"And we'll have to figure out how to get it up here. I'm sure we can pay for some kind of delivery. I'll look into options this week," she volunteered.

"Thank you, dear. I don't know what I'd do without you."

"Back at you," Nicole said, trying not to think about the darkest days when she'd been afraid Adele wouldn't make it. Tears stung her eyes, and she blinked rapidly. She sometimes wondered, in occasional guilty moments, if she'd decided to have the artificial insemination procedure because she was so aware she might lose the person who mattered the most to her. But she'd assured herself that the decision was not merely a reaction to fear. Nicole had wanted to be a mother as far back as she could remember. Some of her earliest memories were singing to and "feeding" baby dolls.

Granted, she'd thought she would be raising children with a husband, but she was almost thirty and couldn't remember the last time she'd gone on more than four dates with the same guy. She still hoped to fall in love and marry someday, but it had begun to seem silly to put her dream on hold, waiting for something that may or may not ever happen. She'd always been the kind of person to take initiative.

And sometimes taking initiative meant giving a friend a swift kick in the tush. Accepting her glass of sparkling juice, Nicole said, "Chris Miller texted me on my way up. I'm going to try to see him and Lizzie this week."

Adele was so still, it didn't even look as if she were breathing. "Well, naturally. I figured you would."

Although Adele had refused to contact her children directly during her chemotherapy, she'd sent Nicole to Dallas with a merger proposal between AB Windpower and Baron Energies. Nicole had never believed the industry giant would link themselves with the much smaller alternative energy company, but it had given her the opportunity to meet Lizzie Baron in person, to report back to Adele that her daughter was savvy and kind and on the verge of motherhood herself. During one of Lizzie and Nicole's meetings, Lizzie had begun cramping and bleeding; it was Nicole who'd driven her to the hospital. Although the women didn't know each other well, Nicole considered Lizzie a friend.

"And you figured I'd let you in on how they're doing? Maybe take a few pictures of the baby?" Nicole asked. Despite her loyalty and affection for her boss, she didn't enjoy feeling like a spy. And she didn't enjoy lying by omission. "I have a better idea. You should make plans to see them for yourself."

Reaching blindly behind her, Adele groped for the cream leather sofa and sank onto it. "Surely you don't think I should call my grown daughter out of the blue and say, 'Hey, can we grab coffee?'"

"Nothing that glib." Nicole sat next to her. "Now that your health is better, you should get in touch with them. Adele, you have a second chance. Don't waste it. I can't keep stalking them. It's creepy."

"It's not as if I asked you to hide in the shrubbery and watch them through binoculars." Adele tried to joke about the situation, but her light tone didn't last long. "What if my reaching out only upsets them? I don't want to intrude where I'm not welcome. Can you…can you ask Lizzie about me, about whether she'd *want* to hear from her estranged mother after all this time? I know she doesn't necessarily speak for all of them, but she's the oldest. When they were little, her sisters looked up to her. Lizzie might be a good barometer of how they feel."

Now that Lizzie's baby was born, conversation about motherhood would be natural. Nicole could ask gentle questions about whether Lizzie missed her own mom. She hoped she'd handle the situation delicately enough; Chris and Lizzie probably weren't getting a lot of sleep these days. Their emotions could be on edge—to say nothing of Nicole's own pregnancy mood swings. She'd been a bit of a tomboy growing up and had almost never cried when she fell off a bike or when her foster brothers teased her about being "too short" to play basketball. Yet for the past week, she'd constantly felt on the edge of tears. Was now really the best time to play mediator?

It's Christmas—the season of miracles. And a miracle may be exactly what Adele and her children needed.

EVERY TELEVISION CHANNEL seemed intent on reminding the viewer that Christmas was around the corner—classic animated movies, Christmas episodes of popular sitcoms, commercials promising "perfect gifts" for loved ones. Daniel Burke Baron punched the power button on the remote with an internal *bah, humbug*. Pain made him cranky. While Texas wasn't known for cold weather, the low temperature tonight was frosty enough to aggravate the lingering ache in his bruised ribs and make his recovering shoulder feel stiffer than normal.

Last month, he'd had surgery after being thrown from a bull in the rodeo ring, and he was damned impatient to get started with physical therapy. He wanted to feel like himself again.

With the television turned off, silence pressed in around him. But it lasted only a moment before a knock resounded through the one-room, remodeled bunkhouse. This building had once been part of a ranch that sold off its acreage to neighboring spreads decades ago. Daniel had wanted something simple, just a comfortable, low-maintenance place to crash when he wasn't out on the rodeo circuit. It was a few miles from the practice ring and livestock on the Roughneck, his stepfather's ranch, but lately Daniel had been wondering if he should have struck farther out on his own.

Annoyed with the fresh throbbing in his side when he stood, he answered the door, unsurprised to find his older brother, Jacob.

In lieu of a greeting, Jacob stated the obvious. "You missed Sunday dinner."

It was traditional for the Baron siblings and step siblings to gather at the ranch on Sunday evenings for a family meal. Those meals had become increasingly crowded lately. Two of his stepsisters had married within the past year. Jet, Carly and Jacob were all engaged. And it wasn't just spouses or fiancés who'd been added to the mix. Until a few months ago, the only kid under the roof had been Alex, the son of Brock Baron's third wife. Now the five-year-old was surrounded by new cousins. Daniel had been as stunned as his brother when Jacob discovered in October that he had a toddler son, but in a very short time, Cody had become the center of Jacob's world.

"Sorry," Daniel said. "Didn't quite feel up to it tonight." If he were being honest with himself, it wasn't just the shoulder pain that had made him reluctant to go. This was the time of year he always missed his mother the most, and his seasonal melancholy seemed like an ill fit for all the nuptial bliss around the dining room table. Why dampen everyone else's festive mood?

"Well, Anna sent leftovers." Jacob held out two Tupperware containers.

Daniel's mouth lifted in a half grin. He'd always been fond of the housekeeper. She was like him, a member of the household, but not exactly a Baron. Although Brock had adopted Daniel and Jacob after marrying Peggy Burke, he'd never treated them as entirely equal to his real children.

"Thanks. I haven't actually eaten yet."

Jacob followed Daniel to the kitchen. "The other reason I stopped by was to let you know I found you a replacement chauffeur for tomorrow." Ever since Daniel's accident, Jacob had been driving him to his medical appointments.

"I could drive myself."

"In downtown traffic? That sling on your arm limits your reflexes and range of motion."

They might be adults now, but Jacob was still the same protective big brother who'd tried to look after Daniel when their biological father was arrested for embezzlement and sent to prison.

"I feel bad that I can't reschedule my meeting," Jacob said.

"Don't even *consider* that, not when you worked so hard to get where you are." After years of Jacob busting his ass to earn their stepfather's respect, Brock had finally deigned to give Jacob a position at Baron Energies. "Seriously, I'll survive without the moral support."

Jacob knew better than anyone how much Daniel disliked doctors' offices and hospitals, nearly to the point of phobia, but Daniel was almost looking forward to this visit. If all went well, he'd leave the appointment sling-free and cleared to begin therapy.

After sticking one of the containers in the microwave, Daniel went to the refrigerator for a beer. He offered one to his brother. "You have a few minutes to stick around, or does Mariana need your help wrangling Cody into bed?"

Grinning, Jacob reached for the bottle. "The nice thing about time at the ranch is that Cody wears himself out. Lots of space to run around, lots of kids to play with. He was asleep when I dropped off him and Mariana at the house. And speaking of being dropped off…Carly's going to drive you to your orthopedic appointment. She has a dress fitting four blocks away, so it just makes sense. She'll come back and get you afterward."

Carly was the youngest of the Baron sisters and a real spitfire. Barrel racing hadn't been enough for her; she'd also insisted on trying her hand at bull riding. But lately, her conversations were less about rodeo standings and more about flower arrangements and seating charts. She was getting married at the end of December, just after Christmas.

"So was dinner conversation all about weddings?" Daniel asked. Next spring, he'd be standing as Jacob's best man. He should probably come up with some helpful input between now and then.

Jacob frowned. "Actually, when Brock was out of the room, talk was mostly about Delia. I mean, Adele."

For months now, Daniel's stepsiblings had been working to find out what happened to their mother, Delia Baron. They'd learned that she'd changed her name to Adele Black and was in fact the CEO of AB Windpower. Now that they knew who she was, they'd been trying to agree on how to proceed. They were troubled by the discovery that she'd been buying chunks of Baron Energies stock. Daniel had the impression that Savannah and Carly in particular wanted to reunite with their estranged mom, but it would be difficult to find a happy ending if she was trying to orchestrate some kind of takeover.

Frankly, Daniel's adolescence—his father's arrest and, later, his mom's death—had left him skeptical about happy endings in general.

Stifling his cynicism, he carried his food to the table and changed the subject to an upcoming rodeo exhibition, a charity event to raise funds for youth programs. If Daniel hadn't been injured, he would have participated. As it was, he planned to attend to cheer on some buddies and talk others into buying tickets for a good cause.

As they chatted about mutual rodeo acquaintances, Jacob suddenly snapped his fingers. "I've been meaning to tell you—Bodie Williams is in town." Another veteran of the rodeo circuit, Bodie had been a friend to both brothers. He'd never made it as high in the standings as Jacob or Daniel, though, and had quit for full-time ranch work.

Daniel lowered his gaze, feeling suddenly guilty. "Yeah. Actually, he and I caught up at a sports bar Friday afternoon." Bodie had shown him pictures of the ranch in Colorado where he worked. The Double F was hiring, and Bodie was willing to put in a good word on Daniel's behalf with his new boss.

If Daniel admitted that he was thinking about leaving, would Jacob support the move or try to talk him into staying? The two of them had always been close. After their mom's death, they'd shared a kind of "us against the world" bond. But Jacob was raising a son now. He worked for the family company, had been accepted into the fold and would be married by this time next year. His life was moving forward in a clear direction.

Daniel, on the other hand, felt increasingly out of place. For a while, success in the rodeo arena had given him some common ground with the other Barons. But between his injury and the way his siblings had been falling in love left and right…

New Year's was just around the corner. Wasn't that a perfect time for resolutions and fresh starts? Maybe Daniel's fresh start was in Colorado.

Chapter Two

After a morning of phone tag and realizing that her friends were nervous about taking a baby out among holiday crowds, Nicole offered to meet Chris and Lizzie for lunch at their own home. It had seemed like a simple, low-stress solution.

The Millers were both dark-haired and attractive, a well-matched couple. But right now, they both wore similar strained expressions. Nicole sat at the kitchen table, trying not to wince.

"She's not usually this fussy," Lizzie said apologetically, pacing laps around the kitchen and trying to soothe the shrieking infant in her arms. "She should be napping, but she's too tired to fall asleep."

Chris, who'd been pulling bowls out of a cabinet for their soup, studied his wife with protective concern. "You look like you could use a break. Why don't you let me take her for a bit?"

Lizzie passed along the pink-clad bundle, then got an oven mitt to lift the hot lid off the slow cooker. The tantalizing scent of homemade ham and bean soup filled the room.

It smelled delicious, but Nicole felt guilty that the

two busy parents had gone to any trouble. "I wish you'd let me bring something from the deli." In the next room, Natalie was still crying, but it seemed less vehement now.

Lizzie shook her head. "The soup was easy, I swear. And I'm not used to spending so much time at home. Don't get me wrong, I adore the time with my daughter, but I still need to feel useful in other ways."

During a lull in the crying, they could hear the low murmur of Chris's voice as he sang to the infant.

Cocking her head, Lizzie paused to listen. "He is so good with her." There was a wealth of love in her voice. Despite any frustrations like a baby who wouldn't stop crying or the drastic changes to Lizzie's schedule, she was obviously happy with her life. "Sometimes it's hard to believe I'd planned to be a single mother. When I first told Chris I was pregnant, I wasn't sure how involved he'd want to be—we weren't exactly together at the time. But now, I can't imagine my life without him. I don't know how women do this alone."

Nicole swallowed hard. Raising a baby on her own was a daunting prospect. But people did it all the time, her own mother notwithstanding. Financially, Nicole was more fortunate than many, and she could afford to hire help. She hadn't made this decision with the naive belief that it would be easy; she'd simply refused to let fear stop her from pursuing what she most wanted out of life.

"You okay?" Lizzie asked, jolting Nicole from her thoughts.

"Sure. Sorry. Distracted by work stuff," she lied.

Something shifted in Lizzie's gaze, as if she were holding back a comment.

"What is it?" Nicole prodded.

"I… Maybe we should wait for Chris to come back. He was going to handle this."

"Handle what?" Nicole asked, her curiosity now at peak level.

"Part of the reason we wanted to see you was to ask you about…" She sighed. "I don't want to put you in a difficult position. AB Windpower is your employer. More specifically, Adele Black is your employer. I understand your loyalty is to her."

There was a shaky, emotional emphasis on the *her*. Lizzie didn't sound as if she were just talking about a CEO of another energy company. Oh, God. Did Lizzie *know* Adele was her mother? Nicole hadn't been prepared for that. If Lizzie confided in her, should Nicole admit she was already aware of the situation? That she'd known Adele's relation to the Barons even before meeting Lizzie?

By nature, Nicole was a forthright person. Skirting the truth didn't come easily to her. Right now, she felt as if she were wearing a blinking neon sign that said Deception! Ulterior Motives! Rising Nausea!

That last part overwhelmed her out of the blue. She closed her eyes, breathing deeply and willing it to pass. "Can you excuse me for a minute? I need to use the restroom." She fought her instinct to sprint through their house, but only barely. She passed Chris at an impressive speed-walking clip.

Though the baby's cries had tapered, she was still putting up a fight. As Nicole pressed cold water to her face, she heard another howl. She could empathize. If she had to choose between allegiance to Adele and friendship with the Millers, she might cry, too.

DR. GREENE, A TALL, slim woman in her fifties, raised her eyebrows above her wire-rim glasses. "You're awfully tense. Worried about the results of the surgery?"

Daniel shook his head, feeling sheepish. "Medical facilities give me the heebie-jeebies. No offense, Doc."

"None taken." She confirmed that he was doing the "passive" exercises she'd recommended and that he could make it through most days without pain medication. "All things considered, you're healing nicely. But…even with the surgical reattachment of the ligament and the physical therapy you'll be starting, your shoulder's stability is compromised. I have a son your age. And if he were in the same situation, I'd ask him to think about quitting the rodeo circuit. Going forward, you're in jeopardy of reinjuring your shoulder."

The idea of giving up rodeos wasn't as upsetting as she might think. Although Daniel had worked hard to earn his ranking—sometimes even beating Jacob, who'd had a real shot at the National Finals—his career path had developed more from his environment than a conscious desire on his part. People called oil the family business, and God knew Baron Energies had made Brock plenty of money, but, until this year, it would have been equally true to say rodeo was the family business.

His thoughts drifted to Bodie's description of life at the Double F. Daniel enjoyed physical labor. Ranch work would allow him to continue being around livestock without the risks of trying to stay on Brahman or longhorn descendants specifically bred to buck.

Thanking the doctor for her advice, Daniel promised to give it serious consideration. She told him he could pick up the referral paperwork for the therapist at the checkout window, then left him to put his shirt back on. He was glad not to be hampered by the sling anymore, anxious to start PT and rebuild his strength.

When he returned to the waiting room, he spotted Carly in one of the padded seats, idly twisting a blond curl around her finger as she studied a bridal magazine. As he got close enough to see the hot-pink headline, he realized she was looking at a checklist. Damn, there were a lot of items! Surely checklists that detailed were necessary only for royal weddings.

She glanced up with a smile. "All done?"

"Finished and sling-free."

"Great. Do you mind if we make a stop on the way to your place? I need to swing by the florist and double-check all the arrangements. And corsages. And bouquets. I'd love to get your opinion on them!" She paused, then flashed a mischievous smile at his rising discomfort. "Kidding. Julieta asked me to drop off some assorted baby supplies Chris and Lizzie left at the ranch yesterday."

Midday traffic wasn't too bad, and the drive didn't take long.

As Carly grabbed the baby stuff from the backseat, she asked, "Aren't you coming in? I mean, I don't expect to be here long, but I was going to take the opportunity to snuggle our niece. Assuming she's awake."

He'd already missed a family gathering yesterday.

Staying in the vehicle now would be downright antisocial. A few feet from the front door, it became evident that baby Natalie was very much awake.

"Yikes." Carly grimaced. "Someone's unhappy."

Daniel wondered if, among the metric ton of other infant-care paraphernalia, Chris and Lizzie had also purchased earplugs.

Without bothering to knock, Carly opened the door. "Hello?" They found Chris in the living room, pacing with his daughter. "I brought some of the things you guys left at the Roughneck. Any chance there's something in this bag that will help? Favorite pacifier? Magic wand?"

"I think this'll be over soon," Chris said. "She can't even keep her eyes open. It's not the most peaceful way to fall asleep, but she'll be out in another ten minutes."

Ten more minutes of this? Daniel felt a wave of sympathy for the other man.

Chris nodded toward the kitchen. "Lizzie was just about to fill some bowls of soup if you guys haven't eaten lunch yet."

"Thanks, but I had a big breakfast," Carly said. Daniel could have hugged her for declining the invitation. "But I definitely want to say hi before we leave."

The first thing Daniel noticed as they approached the kitchen was the warm, savory smell. But that was immediately overshadowed by the staggering tension in the room. Lizzie was standing at the counter, holding a ladle in a white-knuckle grip, her eyes bright with emotion.

Seated at the table was another woman, a beautiful brunette who looked vaguely familiar. But if he'd met her before, why didn't he recognize her? Short of being kicked in the head by a bull and sustaining brain damage, it seemed impossible any man would forget her. She was stunning, with something indefinably exotic about her appearance. Perhaps her coloring, or the shape of her dark eyes? Her delicate features were balanced by her lush mouth and framed by thick, straight hair that tumbled well past her shoulders.

Right now, however, her lovely features were crinkled into an anxious frown. Were the two women distraught over the baby's misery, or had he and Carly walked in on the middle of an argument?

"Daniel, Carly." Lizzie cleared her throat, forcing a smile as she met her sister's gaze. "This is Nicole Bennett."

Right! "We met in April," Daniel recalled, "when you brought Lizzie to the hospital."

Nicole nodded. "Nice to see you again."

He would have remembered sooner but he'd been preoccupied when they met, worried about Lizzie. He'd always had a soft spot for the oldest Baron. If anyone could understand Brock's favoritism of Jet and how it made Jacob and Daniel feel, it would have been her. Although she was the firstborn, Brock often underestimated her because she was female. It had taken the old man's medical leave from Baron Energies for him to finally trust her with the responsibility she deserved.

Carly straightened, her posture alert. "Nicole Bennett who works for AB Windpower?"

No wonder the atmosphere was tense. Had Chris and Lizzie invited the woman here to ask her about the stock purchases?

Whatever conversation had been taking place, Nicole looked reluctant to continue. She rose from her chair. "I should get back to the office."

"We haven't even had lunch," Lizzie protested.

"I wouldn't have eaten much anyway," Nicole said. "My, um, stomach hasn't entirely settled since the turbulent flight into Dallas yesterday. I don't blame the baby for having an off day, but I'm not sure this is the best time to talk. It sounds like you and Chris wanted to ask me some questions. Instead of trying to cram everything into my lunch hour, why don't we get together over the weekend?"

"I'd like to be there, too," Carly said softly. "Sorry. I realize you don't know me, but—"

"Actually, I think you *should* be present for the conversation," Nicole agreed. "Probably Savannah and Jet, too."

Wow. Her bravery was impressive. Facing down all the Barons at once was no easy task.

"Are you free Sunday?" Lizzie asked. "You could join us at the ranch."

Daniel's eyebrows shot up. Nothing like trial by fire. "What is that, like ten against one?"

All three females turned to him in surprise. Well, he was surprised, too. He hadn't meant to voice his thoughts.

"Nobody's 'against' Nicole," Lizzie said, a hint of indignation in her voice. "She's right, though. We do have some questions for her." The Baron sisters exchanged glances, then Lizzie added, "But there's no reason we have to ask them in front of Dad. After everyone's done eating, he can take the older kids to feed the goats or something."

"Just text me what time and let me know what I can bring," Nicole said. "Dessert? A loaf of French bread?"

"Just answers," Lizzie said, her expression forlorn.

Instead of looking cornered or dreading the inevitable interrogation, Nicole stepped forward and squeezed her hand. "I'll answer anything I can, I promise. Guess I'll see all of you this weekend?" She shot Daniel a questioning glance.

Nodding, Daniel had the fleeting thought that maybe his presence would give Nicole a measure of moral support. *Ridiculous.* She barely knew him. Besides, if she confirmed that Adele Black was in some way attempting to damage Baron Energies, there wasn't much Daniel could do to stop the outrage headed her way. Watching her leave, he silently wished her good luck.

When he turned back, he found both his stepsisters regarding him with speculative expressions. For the first time since he'd arrived, Lizzie didn't look upset. In fact, her lips twitched in the beginning of a smile. She and Carly exchanged knowing glances.

And Daniel experienced a stab of foreboding.

NICOLE MADE A beeline to the small meeting room Adele was using as an office, sparing a moment from her anxiety attack to appreciate that her friend even felt well enough to come into work. There had been times during the past two years when that had been the exception rather than the rule.

Adele glanced up from the spreadsheet printouts she was going over with one of the local employees, her smile faltering when she saw Nicole's expression. "Everything okay?"

"Absolutely. I just need to run something by you when you have a minute."

"We were finishing up here." She smiled at the bearded man who sat next to her. "Nice job. If there's nothing else…?"

"Nope, we covered everything." He straightened his Christmas tie and reached for the suit jacket hanging on the back of his chair. It was very warm in here. Adele, who got cold easily these days, had an electric heater plugged in a few feet away. The man nodded politely to Nicole, then headed down the hall.

Closing the door for privacy, Nicole took a deep breath. *We have a problem.* But she swallowed back the words, wanting to put a positive spin on the situation. Would it really be so terrible if Lizzie had figured out that Delia Baron and Adele Black were the same woman? Whatever mistakes she'd made in the past, Adele was a wonderful person. The Baron siblings deserved to know their mother and vice versa.

The biggest drawback she could see to Lizzie and the others knowing Adele's identity was that Adele had been robbed of the opportunity to tell them herself. They might question whether she would have come forward of her own volition.

Nicole dropped into a chair, amazed she could be this tired so early in the day. There had been points in her career when she'd worked until ten o'clock at night without even realizing it. Now she felt as if she needed a nap by two in the afternoon. The half dozen pregnancy books loaded onto her e-reader said exhaustion was normal in the first trimester and often passed. Still, she'd feel better if she could get that confirmed from someone who'd been through it recently. She desperately wanted to confide in Lizzie, but it would be wrong to tell her before Adele, who'd known Nicole for so much longer and given her so many opportunities.

"Did you see Chris and Lizzie?" Adele sat forward in her chair, showing her eagerness for any scrap of information about her daughter.

"I did. They invited me to their house, but we cut lunch short. Your granddaughter is even more beautiful in person than in the pictures Chris emailed me." There'd been a moment when Nicole first arrived, before the crying started, when Natalie had looked so angelic that tears had pricked Nicole's eyes. "She also has a healthy set of lungs on her. Her resistance to falling asleep made conversation difficult, so we rescheduled for Sunday. But, Adele, I'm afraid Sunday could get a little tricky."

"How do you mean?"

"Lizzie said she had questions for me, but she didn't know how to ask because she knows I'm loyal to my employer. To you. She looked…shaken up. And she's not someone who rattles easily. I think she and Carly and the others may have figured out that you're their mother."

So many emotions flashed across Adele's face that it was almost dizzying to watch. Joy and terror and disbelief and hope. "I don't know what to say." She hugged her arms around herself. "I suppose I always knew it was a possibility, but as the years passed, it seemed less and less likely. I wasn't sure that, after what I did, they'd care enough to look."

Had they gone searching for their mom, or had it been more of an accidental discovery? Considering Adele's name change, the latter seemed unlikely.

"You know you're one of the most important people in my life," Nicole said, "professionally *and* personally. But I care about Chris and Lizzie, too. I don't want to lie to them." Last spring, she'd respected Adele's wishes, surreptitiously gathering information to assure Adele her kids were thriving, because she hadn't seen the point in upsetting a pregnant Lizzie with news of a mother who was wasting away from cancer. But circumstances were different now.

"You want to tell them who I am on Sunday. Or, if you're right about them knowing, confirm it?"

"That's one option. The other is that perhaps you could get in touch with them yourself before then," Nicole said gently.

"Oh, I don't know. I…" It took her a few seconds to compose herself enough to continue speaking. "You described Lizzie as 'shaken up.' Not hopeful or wistful. She may not want to hear from me. And could you blame her? Walking away from those kids was a terrible, terrible thing."

"You had extreme postpartum depression," Nicole said. "You weren't entirely in your right mind."

"Which is why I met with their father later and asked for visitation rights."

Which he'd ruthlessly denied. Brock was a powerful, unyielding man with enough money to fund a team of lawyers. Instead of drawing her children into an ugly legal battle, Adele had left them in peace to bond with their new stepmother.

"I didn't fight hard enough for them," Adele said, her voice low and full of shame. "I could have reached out to them once they were no longer minors, but... how could I face them after all that time? How can I face them now?"

"For what it's worth," Nicole said, "if my own mom tracked me down, I'd want to see her. I'd like to think I've forgiven her for doing what she thought was in my best interest."

Gina Marie Bennett, a pregnant teenager, had angered her parents by not putting her baby up for adoption. As soon as she turned eighteen, they kicked her and Nicole out of the house. Two years later, burdened with a drug problem and a malnourished toddler, Gina Marie had sought refuge in a church during a devastating thunderstorm. For a decade, Nicole had bounced between foster care and an intermittently sober Gina Marie.

Her mother hadn't shown up for a scheduled visit on Nicole's fourteenth birthday. Nicole had held out hope that her mother would eventually return, that they could be a family. But she'd never seen her mom again. When Nicole was sixteen and living in a different home, she received a forwarded Christmas card with no return address. In it, her mother had written that her beautiful daughter deserved a better life than a druggie could provide. Gina Marie had loved her enough to get rid of her, but not enough to stay clean for her.

Now, looking at Adele, Nicole's eyes misted. *What a*

pair we are. One woman who had been dumped by her mom and another who'd walked away from her kids. It didn't take a psychology degree to see how they'd helped fill certain holes in each other's life. But maybe Adele didn't have to settle for a stand-in daughter. Her biological children had never been more in reach.

"If nothing else, you should tell them you're sorry," Nicole added. "It would be good for them and for you."

Adele bit her lip, unconvinced. "I don't want to clear my own conscience at the expense of upsetting them. I know I've already asked far more of you than is appropriate, but can you do me one more favor? When you see them on Sunday, let them know I'm in Dallas, that I'd give anything to see them. But the choice is theirs. If they prefer, I can fade away like I was never here."

Nicole had been Adele's emissary in hundreds of professional situations. She had mixed feelings about serving that role in this capacity, but if there was any chance she could help reunite a family...

"Okay." She prayed that she was right about Lizzie and the others wanting a second chance with their mother. If not, Adele would be crushed.

Meanwhile, since Nicole was being so vocal about her friend coming clean and sharing her secrets, maybe it was only fair she take her own advice. "Just so you know, there's one other thing I want to discuss with Lizzie on Sunday. But I can't imagine telling her—or anyone else—before first telling you. I'm..."

The word was momentous. She paused, struck anew by the magnitude of her choice. Happiness spread through her, a buzz of warmth and excitement. "I'm pregnant."

Adele's eyes widened. She opened her mouth, but no words came out.

"So, I guess it's safe to say you weren't expecting that?" Nicole's queasiness and unusual lack of energy would have eventually given her away, but since she'd been in Dallas for only a day, there hadn't been enough opportunity for Adele to notice yet.

"N-no, definitely not! I have to admit, I've worried at times that taking such good care of me didn't leave you any room for dating. I—"

"The only 'date' involved in conceiving this baby was the cozy night I spent sitting by the fireplace and reading donor files. Well, and the day I had the procedure done, of course."

"Procedure? You were artificially inseminated?" Adele's shock didn't seem to be abating.

"Why not?" Was there a touch of defensiveness in her tone? She dropped a hand to her still-flat abdomen. "I don't know what the future has in store for me, but I know I'm ready to be a mom. Guy or no guy in my life, I want this." Unlike Nicole's younger self, this baby would never, ever feel unwanted. He or she would be completely secure in Nicole's love. "Be happy for me?"

"Of course I am, dear!" The confusion and surprise in Adele's expression faded. "You're going to make a wonderful mom. And if there's anything I can do to help along the way, to repay you for—"

"There's nothing that needs repaying," Nicole insisted. Taking care of Adele hadn't been a selfless act. It had allowed Nicole to feel as if she had some measure of control, even if it was only an illusion. Watching her friend go through that terrible illness had been wrenching, but it would have been even worse if Nicole had felt useless. Cooking Adele doctor-recommended foods and coaxing her to eat had made Nicole feel like a member of the team, as if she was doing her part— no matter how small—to help beat back the cancer.

"A baby." Adjusting to the idea, Adele grinned delightedly. "You do know that, as honorary grand-mother, I'm going to spoil the kid rotten?"

"I'm sure she, or he, will learn a lot from you. God knows I have."

There was no question that Adele would make a wonderful honorary grandmother. But Nicole hoped that by the time her child was born in seven and a half months, Adele would already have plenty of practice with her other grandchildren.

Chapter Three

There was a certain kind of soreness Daniel found gratifying—the kind that came from a challenging workout or staying out all night dancing with pretty ladies. As he exited the therapy building Thursday afternoon, he felt sore but upbeat. His physical therapist had not been what he expected. A gorgeous redhead, Sierra Bailey had a face like a porcelain doll and the soul of a drill sergeant.

After explaining the pendulum exercises she wanted him to do at home, she'd warned, "I'll know if you don't do them. And there will be hell to pay."

He believed her. He also believed she was eminently qualified to whip him back into shape. The plan was to start with a regimen that increased his range of motion and flexibility. Strength would come later. Sierra had told him that once he'd regained enough mobility, she'd add biceps exercises. He couldn't wait to feel like his old self again. He might even spend some extra time at the Roughneck so he could use the ranch's heated pool for some of his exercises.

As he turned onto the sidewalk that cut through the medical complex toward the parking lot, he spotted a dark-haired woman coming from the other direction. She had a hand against her midsection, and his first thought was that she might be in pain. Then the wind tossed her hair back, away from her face. Nicole Bennett? Unlike the tension he'd glimpsed in her face the other day, now she wore a dreamy expression. She radiated a serenity he wasn't sure he personally had ever experienced.

"Nicole?" he called.

She looked up, startled. He felt a twinge of guilt for disrupting her moment of peace. "Daniel." Her voice was breathier than he remembered.

"Did you have an appointment here?" He circled his finger, indicating the horseshoe cluster of buildings that housed medical professionals ranging from orthodontists to podiatrists. Didn't Nicole live in San Antonio? It seemed odd she would have a doctor in Dallas. Not that it was any of his business.

"Oh." She blinked. "I, um…"

"Sorry. Didn't mean to pry. I was just surprised to run into you. I was meeting with my physical therapist for the first time."

Nicole cocked her head, studying him. "Chris mentioned you were hurt bull riding. Was it bad?" Her dark eyes were still roving over his body, ostensibly checking for injury, but his hormones didn't seem to care about the platonic reason for her scrutiny. Awareness simmered through him, clouding his thoughts to the point where he could barely remember her question.

"Whoops." She dropped her gaze. "Guess I'm the one prying now."

"No, that's okay. I…" Got distracted. By her eyes.

Maybe best not to say that to a near stranger. "My injury was bad enough to need outpatient surgery. I consider myself lucky. Could have been a lot worse. Brock's living proof of that." It was ironic, given their many differences, that he and his stepfather had this one thing in common—being knocked on their butts by an ornery bull.

"When I visited Dallas in April, he was in a wheelchair. He's better now?"

"He's back on his feet, but I don't think Julieta's going to let him enter any more senior rodeos."

"What about you? Do you plan to get back in the saddle?"

"I haven't made up my mind, but…probably not." It was easier to admit that to a virtual stranger than his rodeo-centric family. "I enjoyed competing. I *love* winning. But I'm ready for something new. I've been thinking a lot about my future lately, trying to decide what I want to be when I grow up," he joked. "Sometimes you reach a point when it's time to take the next step in your life, you know?"

"I do." Something flickered in her eyes, and she took a deep breath, as if trying to steady herself.

"Are you okay?" He wouldn't be surprised if the idea of facing all the Barons this weekend was giving the poor woman an ulcer.

"Absolutely. But I should be getting back to my office."

"Right. See you Sunday." He lifted his hand in a brief wave, but it quickly became apparent that, although they'd been coming from opposite directions, they were both headed to the same section of the parking lot. The silence between them as they fell in step frayed his nerves.

He couldn't help feeling as if Nicole was headed into the lion's den on Sunday. Growing up on the ranch, he'd had Jacob as an ally. He wanted Nicole to feel she had someone in her corner, too.

"I realize it's not my place to say this," he began, "but there's some history between your employer and the Barons. I don't want you to be caught in the middle. Adele Black, she…" *Now what, genius?* The rest of his unfinished sentence was a Pandora's box he shouldn't open.

"Adele is their mother," Nicole said quietly.

His shoulders slumped in relief. "You know." If it was information she already possessed, then he hadn't crossed any lines by addressing the subject.

She nodded. "And now you've answered my question about whether or not Lizzie and the others know. I was already planning on having a very candid conversation with them, but it's nice to have an idea of what I'm walking into." She was back to studying him—this time, searching his gaze with naked curiosity. "I'm surprised you brought it up, though."

So am I. He'd made it a policy to stay out of discussions about Brock's first wife. But he hadn't wanted Nicole to show up at the ranch unprepared. Did that make him disloyal to his stepsiblings? "Well, the Barons can be intense. They—"

"They? Not 'we'?" She gave him a teasing smile. "Aren't you a Baron, too?"

"On paper." Daniel had wondered more than once if his mom had asked Brock to adopt her boys to provide another layer of insulation between them and convicted felon Oscar Burke. No one at their new school would dare bully a Baron. "I mean, my brother, Jacob, and I are technically Barons, but we weren't born into it. Lizzie and Carly and the others are great. But as kids, with immature sibling rivalry and the awkwardness of meshing two households…"

"I get it. I was a foster kid and lived with some nice families through the years. But even with the ones I felt closest to, they weren't really *my* family."

Hearing about her upbringing made him feel ungrateful. At least he and Jacob had always had a home, always had each other. Who did Nicole Bennett have?

She stopped next to a compact car that sported a decal logo for a well-known rental company. "This is mine, temporarily anyway. Thank you for looking out for me." She surprised him by reaching out, squeezing his forearm gently. At her touch, a rush of endorphins replaced his earlier soreness. He didn't know which he was enjoying more—the contact between them or the way she was looking at him. Her admiring expression did more to make him feel like a badass than any rodeo buckle he'd ever won. "I'm glad you'll be there this weekend, Daniel."

Something shorted in his brain when she said his name, and he heard himself ask, "Would you like a ride? Sunday, obviously. Not now." *What are you doing?* He lived five miles from the ranch and had been trying to stay out of his siblings' investigation of their mom. So why was he volunteering to go completely out of his way to pick up Adele's second-in-command?

She chuckled. "Is this because you feel sorry for me?"

"No, ma'am." If she thought pity was the only reason a man would want to spend time with her, she clearly didn't own a mirror. "I, uh, wasn't supposed to drive much after my fall, so I've been having to rely on volunteer chauffeurs. It feels so good to be in the driver's seat again, I'm looking for excuses to get behind the wheel." Thank God Jacob couldn't hear him now. He'd never let Daniel live down such a lame excuse.

"Plus, GPS isn't always reliable out in rural areas," he continued, powering through the embarrassment. Rodeo taught a man to hang on tight and keep going. "If you ride with me, there's no chance of getting lost, with the added bonus that you know there'll be a friendly face as soon as you arrive."

"I'd like that." She met his eyes, and color tinged her cheeks. "I'd like that a lot."

They exchanged phone numbers and she typed the address where she was staying into his contact list. Daniel climbed into his truck, whistling under his breath and unable to remember the last time he'd been so eager for one of the weekly family gatherings.

"YOU ARE A bad influence," Nicole chided, leaning back in her chair. "We should be at the office."

Adele grinned. "I notice you didn't let guilt stop you from enjoying that giant cinnamon roll." It had been Adele's idea to sneak away from work early and window-shop at the extravagant Galleria. They'd covered much of the first two floors before Adele's energy began to flag. Nicole had suggested they get a snack and watch the ice skaters on the rink below. Amateurs wobbled around the edge of the oval while a few standouts in sparkly leotards and skirts executed athletic spins in the center.

Truthfully, Nicole probably should feel guiltier about leaving the office. She'd already missed an hour that morning when she'd interviewed the new OB. Thinking about how Adele had gotten a second medical opinion here in Dallas, Nicole had realized she should probably get a backup obstetrician. Since traveling wasn't generally prohibited until the last trimester, she might spend a good chunk of her pregnancy here. It would be smart to have someone local who knew her history. She'd liked Dr. Davis and had scheduled an ultrasound with him for next week. She couldn't wait to see the first sonogram photograph, even though she knew the earliest pictures weren't discernible as babies.

"Thinking about the baby?" Adele asked.

"How'd you know?"

Adele looked pointedly at Nicole's stomach, where her hand rested. "A lot of pregnant women fall into the unconscious habit of doing that. As if we need some way to commune with the babies before we can feel them moving, as if it makes them more real somehow."

Even knowing Adele's history, it was still difficult to remember sometimes that she'd gone through four pregnancies.

"So everything went all right at the doctor's?" Adele asked.

"Fine. He didn't examine me today. This was more of a quick meet and greet to fill out all the paperwork and make sure I was comfortable with him. You'll never believe who I ran into—Daniel Baron."

Adele blinked. "At the OB-GYN's?"

"No. Outside. It's the same health-care complex where he has physical therapy. He mentioned you, confirmed that the Barons know you're their mother."

Adele nodded, unsurprised. After Nicole's suspicions earlier in the week, Adele had discovered her children had definitely been searching for her. She'd even touched base with an old friend, Genevieve Lewis in Lubbock, who said Carly Baron came to visit, asking questions about her long-lost mother.

Swirling her straw around in what was left of her lemonade, Nicole recalled the unexpectedly protective tone in Daniel's voice. *I don't want you to be caught in the middle.* She was touched that he cared. Since Nicole had learned young that people in her life were temporary, she'd spent a lot of years looking out for herself. She wasn't used to feeling as if someone had her back—especially someone she hardly knew.

In fact, she wasn't sure which she found more charming, that he'd gone out of his way to prepare her for a meeting with his family or how he'd stumbled over asking if she wanted to ride with him. Daniel was very tall, with a chiseled jawline and natural swagger. The man routinely dealt with two-thousand-pound bulls, yet *she* had the power to fluster him? Heady thought. It made her feel as if they were even for that moment when they'd first shook hands last spring and she'd barely been able to remember the word *hi*.

Adele stared across the table, her expression shrewd. "Maybe you should tell me more about this Daniel."

"With the way you've tried to keep up with the Barons over the years? You probably know more about him than I do." Even though Daniel wasn't related to the others by blood, Nicole was sure her employer would have wanted at least some data on the guy who'd grown up with her children. "I've only seen him on a handful of occasions."

"Still, I've always respected your instincts. First impression?"

He has incredible green eyes. "I think he has a strong sense of justice, a desire for things to be fair. When Lizzie invited me to the ranch, he objected that they were ganging up on me." Integrity was a good quality, but she wondered how he coped when life was so often unfair. She knew his mother had died when he was still relatively young. And now his rodeo career may be ending right when he was in his prime.

She also knew, from the way he talked about the Barons as "they," that he felt a little like an outsider, but she kept that observation to herself. It was a feeling she'd experienced far too often in her own life. Her first real sense of belonging had come from her promotions at AB Windpower and the connection that had grown between her and Adele.

"I so appreciate the chances you've given me," she said. "Obviously we still have tons of time before I'll need maternity leave, but I want you to know I plan to come back as dedicated as ever."

"First of all, I never gave you anything you didn't earn. As for as the other part… Your job's not going anywhere, and I hope you stay on in a full-time position for years to come. But having a child changes you." Adele glanced out across the skaters, as if she were trying to hide the sadness in her expression. She couldn't disguise the regret in her voice. "Sometimes in ways you never could have predicted or would have believed of yourself."

THE LONGHORN SALOON was doing a thriving business on Friday night. Daniel stepped inside with his brother, wondering if they'd be able to find seats. Jacob waved to someone in the crowd then turned to tell Daniel, "Jet's got us a table already."

Daniel tried not to let his surprise show on his face. He hadn't realized Jet would be joining them.

Jacob paused midstride. "You don't mind that I invited him along, do you?"

Mind? No. But it was a sign of how things were changing, of Jacob's growing ease with their stepsiblings. *Good for him.* Jacob was a hell of a big brother, and he'd fought hard to reach his current state of acceptance and happiness.

"I mentioned it to him before we left the exhibition," Jacob said. They'd passed Jet at the rodeo fund-raiser earlier in the evening.

"It makes sense to get Jet's input," Daniel said casually. "Luke will be his brother-in-law, too."

As the best man for Luke and Carly's fast-approaching wedding, Jacob was supposed to plan the bachelor party. Carly had made laughing threats about what she would do to them if there were strippers involved. Jacob had been thinking in terms of an upscale gambling night with pretty card dealers at the poker and blackjack tables. They were here tonight to brainstorm specifics.

They passed the long bar, with its mirrored wall reflecting the usual crowd on the dance floor and people gathered around the mechanical bull in the corner. One of George Strait's slower songs played on the jukebox, and Daniel found himself randomly wondering if Nicole Bennett liked to dance. It wasn't the first time she'd drifted through his mind since their encounter yesterday.

In fact, he was finding it difficult not to think about her. The executive was beautiful in a different way than most of the women he knew—he couldn't quite picture her in boots and jeans—but her allure went beyond physical. She was smart, sharp enough to work her way to an impressive position for a woman under thirty. Daniel knew that Jacob and Lizzie had busted their respective asses to get Brock to increase their responsibility at Baron Energies, but that kind of success had to be even more difficult when you didn't have a powerful name or family business.

The table Jet had secured was tall and narrow. It was awkward for three men to try to fit around, but Daniel was grateful to have any spot on such a popular night. They ordered a pitcher of beer and chatted about the event they'd just left. From the curious looks both men cast in his direction, he guessed they were silently speculating on whether he'd be returning to rodeo. It was only part of how he made a living, of course. He had also invested in a friend's stock contracting, breeding animals for rodeo, and Daniel stayed busy on the side training horses, although his injury had temporarily limited him to more of a consulting position. He liked everything he did well enough, but there was still a niggling sense of disquiet. As if he hadn't yet found the right fit.

Eventually, the subject turned to Luke and Carly's wedding. "Luke warned me from the start that there would be a lot of details," Jacob said. "This is Carly's big day, and she's nothing if not strong-minded."

Jet and Daniel both grinned at that. When the Burke boys had first moved to the ranch, Daniel had gone through an ill-advised period of getting into trouble. While Brock's aloofness had made Jacob work all the harder to be the best at everything, Daniel had taken the juvenile approach that if the old man wasn't going to like him anyway, Daniel might as well live down to his low expectations. Whereas Savannah was likely to shake her head at his transgressions and turn a blind eye—as long as he wasn't physically endangering himself—and Lizzie, always more responsible than her years, would scold like a miniadult, Carly was busy getting into her own scrapes.

She was a different woman now. He wasn't sure if it was solely the result of mellowing with age or the contentment that came from her relationship with Luke.

"I think all the wedding talk is making Mariana even more anxious for the spring," Jacob added, looking eager himself. He and Mariana were planning a longer engagement than Luke and Carly, but no one could doubt that they were every bit as much in love. "Although, it's hard for her, knowing Leah won't be there to see it."

Mariana's sister—Cody's mother—had died tragically young. Daniel thought his siblings were brave, rushing headlong into new commitments when family so often equaled loss. Who should know that better than the Barons, after they'd been abandoned by Delia and then lost their stepmother?

Jacob clapped Daniel on the back. "I know it wouldn't be the same for me if you couldn't be there."

Naturally, Daniel had agreed to be the best man, but he felt like a bit of a fraud. Maybe the job should go to someone like Jet or Luke, someone who genuinely believed in marriage. Or maybe Daniel should warn Jacob that he was thinking of relocating. Obviously, Daniel would travel from any corner of the earth to be at his brother's wedding, but it might be easier for someone local to handle the wedding-related tasks. Then again, nothing was definite yet, and when the time came to tell Jacob he might be leaving, it should be a one-on-one conversation, not something shared in a noisy bar.

They discussed where and when they could hold the bachelor party and the potential head count. The bride and groom definitely didn't want the festivities to be the night before the wedding; Carly said she wanted guests to have plenty of time to recover from any hangovers. Jacob made some notes on his phone about equipment they'd need to rent and staff they'd need to hire and said he'd talk to Luke about getting a guest list on Sunday.

"About Sunday." Jet tilted his cowboy hat back on his head. "I understand Lizzie and Carly invited Nicole Bennett to join us."

"The woman who works for Adele?" Jacob asked.

"Right, the one who took Lizzie to the hospital that time," Jet said. "Cute, from what I recall." He said the words matter-of-factly with no personal interest. These days, he had eyes only for Jasmine Marks.

"Cute?" Daniel echoed in disbelief.

"You don't think she's attractive?" Jacob asked.

On the contrary. Daniel thought *cute* was far too girlish and tepid to describe her. "I…"

"Do you realize," Jet said, suddenly solemn, "that Nicole has spent more time with my own mother than I have? I'm torn between resenting her and wanting to ask her a hundred dumb questions, like what's Delia— um, Adele's—favorite movie or country singer."

"It's not dumb to want to know more about your mom," Daniel said. The holiday season intensified how much he missed his own mother, and he couldn't help empathizing with the ache in Jet's tone. "But as far as the resentment goes, I hope you won't take Adele's mistakes out on Nicole."

Jacob's eyebrows shot up, and the questioning look he gave Daniel over his mug of beer made Daniel realize how protective he'd sounded.

Jet frowned. "Of course not. I have three sisters. They'd hog-tie me and have me beaten if I was rude to a woman. Jasmine wouldn't stand for it either. Speaking of which…" He checked the time and threw a five-dollar bill on the table. "I have someone waiting for me at home who's a lot prettier than either of you two."

As their stepbrother blended into the crowd, Jacob returned to the topic of Nicole. "How well do you know Nicole Bennett?"

"She's practically a stranger." It was the truth. There was no rational reason for him to have been so concerned about her when he'd found her upset in Lizzie's kitchen. And there was just as little reason for him to have been so happy to see her yesterday.

"Uh-huh."

For the slightest second, it was on the tip of Daniel's tongue to ask what it had been like when Jacob met Mariana, what his first impressions had been, if he'd had any inkling of what she might come to mean to him. Then again, on the day they'd met, Jacob had just been hit with the bombshell that he was a father. So that had probably been uppermost in his thoughts at the time. Plus, Mariana—whose own father had used the rodeo as an excuse to be a deadbeat dad—hadn't exactly approved of Jacob's lifestyle.

And yet somehow they worked through all of that.

Maybe the trick was wanting it enough to make it work, but Daniel was still surprised by their optimism. Both Mariana and Jacob were children of divorced parents, both had experienced the various ways people who mattered could be ripped from your life.

Jacob pulled out his wallet. "We should probably head out, too. I'm sure other people would appreciate the table." He grinned. "And Jet's not the only one with someone pretty waiting up for him."

NICOLE FROWNED AT her reflection. Was it her imagination, or was her cleavage a lot more noticeable than it should have been in the V-necked sweater? She was tempted to pick another outfit—which she'd already done twice. She was going to have an emotional conversation with Adele's children today, and Nicole felt most self-assured in her suit jackets and skirts. But those seemed like ridiculous attire for a family afternoon at the ranch.

She'd shimmied into her favorite pair of jeans, wondering how much longer they'd still fit, and pulled her hair into a ponytail that gave her a more casual appearance. She didn't want to look stiff or as if she were trying too hard. Then again, a little makeup couldn't hurt…

Adele knocked on the bathroom door. "You okay? I can bring you some ginger ale or crackers if your stomach's bothering you."

"My stomach's fine." Nicole cracked the door open and gestured toward the discarded tops on the bathroom counter. "I've been in here so long because I keep changing my mind about which shirt to wear. It's early enough in the pregnancy that changes to my body are probably mostly in my head, but nothing feels entirely comfortable right now."

"And you think that's because of the pregnancy?" Adele looked upward with feigned innocence. "Not, say, because of a certain rodeo cowboy with a 'strong sense of justice'?"

Nicole scowled. "You're mocking me at a time like this? Do you know how nervous I am about facing your family?" The weight of the responsibility, to paint her mentor in a sympathetic light, was crushing. "I really wish you were coming with me."

"I'm not the one they invited." There was a hollowness to her words, and Nicole heard the echo of fear, the worry that Adele would never be welcome.

There was a buzz as Nicole's phone vibrated on the counter, making her stomach pitch and seize. Maybe she should have taken Adele up on those crackers.

"That's Daniel." Nicole picked up her phone, scanning his message that he'd parked and was waiting downstairs. "I told him to text me when he got to the building and I'd meet him in the lobby." It seemed plain wrong for him to meet Adele before her own children were given the chance.

Emotion shone in Adele's damp eyes. "I shouldn't be putting you through this. Especially in your condition. I—"

"You didn't know I was pregnant when you asked me to go to the ranch today. Now, suck it up." Nicole gave her a tremulous smile. "Only one of us can be a wreck at a time."

"I suppose it would be pointless to tell you to have fun?"

"Probably." Nicole tossed her cell phone and lipstick into her purse, checking to make sure she had plenty of peppermints. Sometimes sucking on them helped quell the nausea. Talking to Lizzie and the others would be awkward enough without Nicole having to bolt for the restroom midsentence.

"You have a bit of a drive between here and the ranch," Adele reminded her. "At least try to enjoy Daniel's company on the way."

At the mention of Daniel's name, Nicole's stomach somersaulted again. But this time the sensation wasn't unpleasant at all.

Chapter Four

Since Nicole's sense of smell was on hyperdrive lately, she avoided the elevator except for when she was simply too fatigued to take the stairs. The convenience of riding down wasn't always worth being stuck in an enclosed space with the Gardenia Perfume Woman on the fifth floor or Eats a Ton of Garlic on three. Today, the stairs also gave her an excuse to burn off some nervous energy.

She spotted Daniel, leaning against the wall by the elevator banks, before he saw her. Last time they'd encountered each other, he'd been leaving physical therapy and was dressed like someone going to the gym. Today he wore dark jeans, a white button-down shirt and a cowboy hat. She was tempted not to make her presence known and spend a few more minutes appreciating the picture he made.

Get a grip. Adele was counting on her. How could Nicole facilitate reconciliation between mother and children if she was distracted by lust-addled pregnancy hormones and the way Daniel Baron filled out a pair of Wranglers?

Taking a deep breath, she approached him with the

same composure and welcoming smile she would have used when greeting a businessman. "Hi."

He whipped his head around. "Nicole." One eyebrow lifted. "This is a surprise."

"Weren't you expecting me?" she teased.

"I was expecting Nicole Bennett, executive. I've never seen you out of your work clothes."

She did a double take at his phrasing—and at the idea of Daniel seeing her out of her clothes.

"I mean, I've only ever seen you in your professional wardrobe," he backpedaled. "I was thinking the other day that I couldn't imagine you in jeans."

"You've been thinking about me?" She wished she hadn't asked the impulsive question. What if it led to awkwardness on their long drive?

But he held her gaze, not looking the least discomfited. "Yes, ma'am."

A liquid shiver went through her. He'd joked about not knowing what he wanted to be when he grew up. He should look into narration or recording books on tape. People would pay good money to listen to that low, rich voice.

"Ready to go?" he asked.

Anywhere you want to lead, cowboy. Wow. The pregnancy books really didn't do these hormone surges justice. Nicole couldn't remember the last time her libido had been so supercharged.

It occurred to her that maybe she should enjoy the sensation while she could. She rarely dated now, and she didn't imagine potential suitors would be lining up at her door once her pregnancy became visibly obvious. And after the baby was born? As the single mother of an infant, Nicole suspected she'd be too tired to indulge an active sex drive.

She definitely had some challenging months ahead of her. But for right now, a hot guy with a smile that stole her breath was opening the door for her. The sunshine outside only added to her upbeat mood.

"What a gorgeous day." She fished in her purse for a pair of sunglasses as they crossed the parking lot. "I'm supposed to pick out a Christmas tree this week, but weather like this makes it feel more like spring than December."

"Definitely a lot warmer than it was last weekend," he agreed, unlocking his truck door. "Christmas tree shopping, huh? So you aren't headed back to San Antonio soon?"

She shook her head. "The plan is for me to spend most of December here." After Chris Miller had turned down the chance to run their Dallas office, choosing instead to resign, she'd been running double duty. "We're working on an exciting project out of our Dallas location, making the final plans for a sizable wind farm that will create new jobs."

Her enthusiasm for the project helped her get through the afternoons when pregnancy fatigue tried to sabotage her. "Squaring away the details and handling press coverage will keep me busy for the next week or so. After that, I'm theoretically free to return to San Antonio, but the office is dead the week of Christmas. It makes just as much sense to stay here and spend my holiday with Adele." Assuming the grown Baron children agreed to meet with their mother. If not, Adele would probably retreat to San Antonio for a bleak yuletide.

Daniel tilted his head, regarding her with curiosity as she fastened her seat belt. "You're going to spend Christmas with your boss?"

"She's more than an employer," Nicole said. "She's like family." Was it an insensitive claim, given how much time Adele had missed with her own family? She sighed, hoping that before the day was over she found the words that would help make up for the lost years, the pain Adele had caused her loved ones. "On a scale from one to I-should-just-throw-myself-from-the-truck, how bad do you think this is gonna be?"

His lips quirked in a half smile, but rather than make a glib reassurance, he took the time to think it over. "I don't know," he admitted. "But I'll do what I can to make it as painless as possible."

"You are a really nice guy."

His laugh was short and self-deprecating. "Actually, I'm a cranky loner and recovering troublemaker." He gave her an appraising look. "Maybe you bring out my better qualities."

As Daniel made the last turn before they reached Roughneck property, Nicole was surprising him with the revelation that not only did she own boots and jeans, she'd once mucked stalls.

"One of the foster homes I lived on was a tiny farm—some vegetable crops, two horses and a chicken coop. All of us kids had chores. I can't say I much cared for cleaning out the stalls, but I did enjoy riding Grey. Of the two mares, she was the one deemed more suitable for beginners. She didn't go very fast, but she was sweet."

"Do you still ride?" he asked, wondering if a visit to the stables was in order this afternoon.

She gave a quick shake of her head, her ponytail swinging lightly behind her. He liked it better when she wore her hair down. With nothing to detract from her face, it was too easy to get distracted by her eyes. Or her lips. "Not for years."

"I'd be happy to give you a refresher," he volunteered. "We've got a range of horses at the ranch, including some with gentle temperaments."

Interest flared in her expression, and he thought for sure she was going to take him up on his offer. "Thanks, but…I'd better pass."

He experienced a stab of selfish disappointment. He would have loved the opportunity to help her into the saddle, but he didn't push the issue. She had enough on her mind today.

"So which place did you like more," he asked, "the farm or the house with the solar panels?"

She'd explained earlier on the drive that her interest in alternative energy had stemmed from another foster home. Listening to her talk about being bounced around, he'd felt a sense of connection. Like him, she'd spent a lot of time feeling as if she didn't quite belong. It was clear, though, that her different stops along the way had helped shape the multifaceted woman she'd become.

"It's hard to say. I always figured my favorite place would be the one where someone wanted to keep me forever. For a long time, I assumed that someone would eventually be my mom. But…" She shrugged, fighting to keep her smile in place. "Life doesn't always work out the way you expect, right?"

"That's for damn sure." His throat tightened as he pictured his own mother. It was ridiculous that she hadn't lived long enough to meet her first grandchild, to hug Cody and help Jacob pick out Christmas presents. For years after she'd died, sometimes Daniel would wake up on Christmas morning and get halfway to the tree with his siblings before he remembered that she wouldn't be there.

"Daniel?"

"Sorry. Mind wandered." He wasn't in the habit of confiding what he was thinking, especially when it involved painful emotions. But it seemed cowardly not to tell her the truth when Nicole had been so honest about her own past, sharing both the good and the bad. "Actually, I was thinking about my mother. Her death was such a shock that sometimes I still can't adjust to her being gone."

"How'd she die?" Nicole asked quietly.

"Infection. She checked into the hospital for what should have been a totally routine appendectomy, then…" He tightened his grip on the steering wheel. One day, she'd been a firm but compassionate mom, someone he'd known he could count on; the next, she'd been gone.

"I'm sorry for your loss."

"Thank you. It was a long time ago."

"The past is always closer than we think," Nicole said. "Sneaks up on us when we don't expect it."

"Is that why Adele sent you with that merger proposition last spring? Was her past creeping up on her, making her curious about her children?" Having watched Carly and Lizzie and the others search for their mom, he couldn't help wondering about the situation. But far greater than his interest in Adele was his interest in Nicole and her part in all this.

She hesitated. Maybe he shouldn't have put her on the spot. Then again, it might be a good idea for her to figure out what she wanted to say before she was faced with four Barons who all had questions about their missing mother.

"Adele has regretted leaving her kids for years— decades. But she convinced herself that staying away was better for them in the long run than the upheaval she'd cause by coming back." Nicole's voice broke a little. "My personal experience is that a mom can justify defection if she believes it's in her kid's best interest. Adele's been guilt-stricken over what she did but figured that staying out of their lives was part of her penance. Brock made it clear she wasn't to come anywhere near them."

Daniel grunted, unsurprised by his stepfather's high-handedness. He'd seen Brock intimidate millionaires and hardened cowboys.

"This time last year, Adele was extremely sick. Cancer. Her prognosis wasn't very good. If Baron Energies had accepted our merger offer, I think it could have been beneficial for both companies. It wasn't a joke—I put a lot of time into that proposal. But, yes, I came to Dallas in part to meet with Lizzie, to get information on how Adele's kids were doing and hopefully give Adele some peace of mind in case... Well. You get the idea."

He did. And he could see how much the memory of Adele's illness still upset her. She'd obviously meant it when she said the woman was like family. "But she's all better now?" He hoped so for both Nicole's sake and for his stepsiblings'. To have their mother back in their lives only to lose her to a recurrence of cancer? That would be too cruel. Having watched his own mother buried, Daniel thought his stepsiblings would be better off spared that experience.

"All of her recent tests have shown her to be cancer-free," Nicole confirmed with a smile. "She has a second chance at life. And, if they're open to the idea, a second chance with her kids."

"I can't really speak for them, but they did want to find her. That must mean something." Carly had even spoken wistfully about what it would be like if her mother could see her married, but it wasn't his place to volunteer that information.

They were on Roughneck property now. Daniel drove over a cattle guard and slowed down as dirt and dust flew up from the unpaved road.

"Wow." Nicole watched with awe as the house and outlying buildings came into view.

He'd seen pictures of the original house that had stood here—it had been renovated considerably after the oil strike. He'd heard others call the stone manor house Brock's castle, but when Daniel had first seen the home, it had struck him as something more foreboding. A fortress, maybe. To the left of the house, cars and trucks were parked. It seemed like every month, the number of vehicles increased.

Had any family ever grown as quickly and dramatically as the Barons? It was still difficult to believe that, by the end of this month, Carly would be stepmom to a cute little cowgirl and that even reformed serial dater Jet was settling down.

"Fair warning," he said, "it can get a little chaotic."

She was grinning in anticipation. "But family chaos is the best kind!" At his disgruntled look, she laughed. "So you're not planning to have six kids of your own someday?"

"I don't plan to have kids at all. Not that I dislike them," he added, trying to lessen the harshness of his words. His nephew, Cody, was adorable, but he added so much intensity to Jacob's life, so much fear. Cody had fallen off a bleacher at a rodeo, and Daniel knew the experience had probably taken ten years off his brother's life. "In the abstract, I like them just fine. But I'm not cut out for…all of this." It was a lame way to try to sum up twenty years of not feeling as if he fit in.

Nicole had gone quiet. Given her own upbringing and lack of relatives, was she irritated that the huge, boisterous family had been wasted on someone who didn't appreciate it?

He rounded the truck to open her door for her, but she was already stepping down when he got there.

Offering a smile, he tried to recapture the lighter mood they'd shared when he first picked her up. "C'mon, I'll introduce you to everyone."

Today was one of those days that made it clear why people would want to winter in Texas. The sunshine offset the chilly breeze, and the youngsters were taking advantage of the pretty weather. The front lawn was abuzz with activity. Under Julieta's smiling supervision, children chased each other in a free-form game of tag where everyone seemed to be It at the same time. Carly's future stepdaughter, Rosie, was chasing Alex with a stuffed elephant, giggling when the five-year-old boy pretended to be afraid.

Jet, who had one three-year-old girl on his shoulders and another twirling in circles around him, waved at them. "Look who finally made it! Lizzie and Chris arrived about twenty minutes ago. Y'all are the last to show up. Nice to see you again, Nicole."

She nodded. "You, too. I see you have your hands full," she said, smiling fondly at the girls. She crouched down to ask the name of the one on the ground; the other twin demanded to be let down to meet the new person.

Meanwhile, Savannah stepped off the porch and came toward them. "Daniel! It's great to see you without the sling. How's your shoulder feeling?"

"Not too bad. The therapist isn't exactly Miss Congeniality, but she's got a reputation for getting great results. Savannah, I'd like you to meet Nicole Bennett."

Savannah turned to their guest with a smile. Whatever reservations Savannah had about her estranged mother or AB Windpower's stock purchases, the only thing in her expression was a friendly welcome. "So glad you could join us! Lizzie's feeding the baby on the patio. You and Daniel can join her while we finish getting the food ready."

Daniel knew he was exempt from carrying dishes

and platters of food until his shoulder was 100 percent again. They crossed through the house so others could offer Nicole a quick hello. Then they passed through the French doors onto the spacious patio with multiple tables and an outdoor kitchen that got a lot of use during the spring and summer. Today, a fire had been lit and portable heaters were spaced between the padded wicker chairs and glass-topped tables to ensure everyone was comfortable.

"Nicole, Daniel." Lizzie kept her greeting soft. She'd apparently finished feeding Natalie, who looked nearly asleep.

"You want me to take her inside to the bassinet?" Christopher offered. There was a baby monitor on the table in front of them, so they'd have no trouble telling when she awoke. Based on what he'd heard the other day, Daniel wasn't sure monitors were necessary. If Natalie needed attention, the people in the next county would probably be able to tell.

"In a minute," Lizzie said. "She's almost out. Would you mind bringing me some more water when you come back?"

"How about you?" Daniel asked Nicole. "Can I get you something to drink? If you're nervous, a beer might help," he teased.

"Actually, water's fine for me, too."

"I'll bring a pitcher and a couple of glasses. Then you're both covered," he said. "Be right back."

But no sooner did he set foot in the kitchen than he was ambushed by females.

Julieta poked him lightly in the ribs—thankfully, his uninjured side. "After all these Sundays, I wondered if we would see the day when *you* brought a friend. Nicole's lovely."

"Uh, she's really Lizzie's friend," he corrected. "Lizzie and Chris invited her. I was only the transportation."

"You sure?" Mariana countered. "Because Jacob said you seemed kind of hung up on her."

Mentally throttling his big brother, Daniel rolled his eyes. "Aren't three weddings and two engagements enough for you people?"

Ever the attorney, Mariana folded her arms and smirked. "Deflection is not the same as a denial."

"So. You and Daniel seem to be getting along well." Lizzie grinned encouragingly.

Nicole kept her tone neutral. "He's nice." Very nice. And one day, he'd probably make a great romantic interest for some woman who lived here in Dallas and shared his resistance to having kids. "Just in case you or Chris is harboring any wild matchmaking ideas, you should know I don't have any interest in dating right now. I have…too many other things going on."

"Other things like trying to stealthily buy up Baron Energies stock?"

"What?" The shift in conversation nearly gave Nicole whiplash.

"Sorry. I wanted to catch you off guard so I could get your honest, unvarnished reaction. My dad raised six kids. Watching him, I've learned a thing or two about how to get confessions."

"I don't have anything to confess," Nicole said. At least, not about that. Adele had bought that stock for personal reasons, not as part of a nefarious scheme. "Look, Lizzie, while we've got this moment alone, let me say…yes, Adele is your mom. I didn't know any of her personal history when I started interning for her in college or even for a few years after she hired me. But I was working late one night and came across her crying. It was your birthday. She told me she'd struggled for a long time with depression and that, as a result of her condition, she'd left her children behind."

Lizzie's eyes glistened with emotion, but she didn't interrupt.

"I knew you were her daughter when I came to Dallas last spring, but I hope my keeping her secret doesn't mean we can't be friends." She had a moment of alarm when Lizzie turned her head away. Was the other woman regretting her invitation to have Nicole come to the ranch? "For what it's worth, which may be nothing, my mom left me when I was thirteen. So I know a little bit of what you're going through."

"Would you want to see her if she showed up now?"

"Yes." Nicole didn't have to stop and think it over—she'd thought about it for years.

"Me, too."

The band of tension around Nicole's chest eased. Adele would be overjoyed. Lizzie's words weren't a guarantee of any future relationship, but they were a start.

"I can't imagine any force in the world that would separate me from Natalie," Lizzie said. "I don't understand why my mom did what she did. I remember her, though. She loved us. But after she came home from the hospital with Jet, she just wasn't… She changed.

Whatever she was going through that would make her abandon us must have been awful. I want to see her. I want to give her a chance to meet her granddaughter."

Nicole swallowed, her throat stinging as she thought of her own unborn baby. She vowed to give it all the love she could, but she couldn't offer it much in the way of extended family.

Lizzie leaned forward. "Can I ask you a personal question?"

"Of course." Between Nicole nursing Lizzie's mother through cancer and once taking Lizzie herself to the hospital, they were pretty well past formalities.

"How far along are you?"

"What? I—" Groaning, she ran a hand over her face. "I was cradling my stomach again, wasn't I?"

"And you declined the beer. And you bolted from my kitchen the other day looking like you were about to lose your breakfast—which, incidentally, is a feeling I well remember. And when you look at Natalie, you get this teary, wonderstruck expression. I mean, my kid's definitely the cutest baby in Texas," she said with a twinkle in her eye, "but people don't normally get weepy when they glance at her."

Nicole heaved a sigh of relief. "I'm glad you know. I have about a million questions I want to ask you! Maybe we could get together sometime, just the two of us? I'm only in my second month, so I'm not really telling people yet. But it would be nice to have someone to talk to."

"Congratulations! And I'm not exactly an expert, only having had the one, but I'm happy to share my experiences. Do you have any sonogram pictures yet?"

Nicole shook her head. "I've got my first ultrasound scheduled for later in the week."

"Chris and I didn't realize you were seeing anyone..." She looked abashed that she'd dropped hints about Daniel.

"I'm not. Wasn't. Well, except a fertility specialist. I decided to do this on my own."

Lizzie whistled. "Brave woman. But if anyone can do it..." She smiled. "So, when you said this was a bad time to be dating, you were serious—not just looking for a polite way to tell me you aren't interested in my brother?"

"Right." She thought of the zing she'd experienced when Daniel admitted he'd been thinking about her. Unimportant. With everything else that was going on, everything she had to prepare for, men were definitely not on her radar right now. Not even one as good-looking and disarmingly considerate as Daniel Baron.

Liar, liar... Running a hand over her pants, she surreptitiously scooted her chair farther from the fire pit and hoped Daniel would be back soon with that pitcher of water. Just to be on the safe side.

NICOLE ENJOYED THE meal far more than she could have predicted, eating with gusto. Knowing that Lizzie didn't blame her for any secrets she'd kept, secrets that hadn't been hers to tell, did a lot to restore her appetite. The food was wonderful, the kids were hilarious and listening to Carly and Luke excitedly discuss their upcoming wedding was heartwarming. Though she still wasn't sure how the group conversation about Adele would go, between Daniel, Chris and Lizzie, she felt as if she had allies in her corner.

After everyone had eaten and Anna and Julieta began clearing plates away, Jacob asked his father to help him herd kids on a visit to the stables. It was Nicole's understanding that Brock knew his daughters had made some inquiries about their mom but didn't support the idea of their reestablishing a connection.

Once Brock was gone, others found subtle ways to busy themselves. There was no obvious mass exodus, yet within ten minutes, Nicole found herself alone with Adele's four children, plus Luke and Daniel. She suspected Chris and Travis had left only because their wives were afraid of Nicole feeling overwhelmed.

She shared with them what she'd already outlined for Daniel and Lizzie—Adele was recovering from serious illness, a revelation that left both Carly and Savannah teary-eyed, but that her health had improved, she was currently in Dallas and she very much wanted to see her children. Nicole took care not to sound as if she were making excuses for what their mother had done. There was no erasing the pain of Adele's abandonment. She explained how the postpartum depression hadn't abated with time, only darkened into a more serious depression that actually began to scare her. Adele had felt overwhelmed with the care of four children and unable to confide her "failings" in her larger-than-life husband. Nicole tried not to paint Brock as an unfeeling husband or scapegoat.

"When can we see her?" Carly asked.

"As soon as you're ready," Nicole said. "I'll give you all the numbers—the office, the apartment, her cell."

She knew that as soon as she returned to the apartment tonight and reported to her friend, Adele would be on high alert, waiting for a phone to ring.

"I can't believe she was so sick and we had no idea." Savannah still looked stricken by the knowledge of her mother's disease.

"I don't want to waste another day," Carly said. "I want to talk to her."

Jet looked somewhat less eager. Though he'd been funny during dinner, a clear extrovert, he'd grown solemn while Nicole talked about his mother. He was the youngest Baron sibling, the one whose birth had preceded Adele's depression. Did he blame himself or wonder if he was partially responsible for the others losing their mom? Or perhaps he just had fewer good memories of her than his sisters.

"Maybe you girls should see her first," he said, forcing a smile. "Mother-daughter bonding time. All four of us together might be a bit much."

As if she'd been watching from inside and could sense her fiancé needed her, pretty blonde Jasmine Marks stepped out onto the patio. "The other ladies sent me to find out if anyone's ready for dessert or coffee."

Daniel rose from his chair. "I'll go round up the kids and let them know it's sugar time. Nicole, would you like to come with me? It'll give you a chance to see more of the ranch."

And it would give her some time to decompress after an emotionally draining conversation. She shot him a grateful smile. He hadn't said much while she talked to the others, but she'd been hyperaware of his presence, his nods of encouragement and supportive glances. It was a shame Daniel didn't want children because she could imagine that quiet, steady reassurance coming in handy while teaching a kid to ride a bike or add fractions.

"I'd love to see more of the ranch," she said.

They walked in companionable silence, which she appreciated. Jacob and Brock met them halfway, already on their way back to the house. When Jacob's son, Cody, heard that dessert was being served, he let out an excited whoop and tugged his dad's hand, urging him to hurry.

"We'll be along in a bit," Daniel said. "Thought I'd show Nicole around first. But save us some pie. Or at least a couple of brownies."

Jacob gave a snort of laughter. "With that horde? I make no promises."

Now that the sun was beginning to set, the air around them felt a lot more like winter. Nicole wrapped her arms around herself, and Daniel noticed.

"You're cold. Do you want to follow them back?"

"Not yet. It's so peaceful out here."

"Sorry I don't have a jacket to offer you."

She imagined snuggling into a coat warm from his body, enveloped in his scent. Since she was daydreaming, why stop there? He could heat her up a lot faster by enfolding her in his arms. She sighed. *Knock it off, Nic.* She'd seen the speculative matchmaking gleam in Lizzie's eyes earlier. It would be sheer folly to encourage that.

They passed two barns and a corral, stopping by a practice ring where Daniel said he and his siblings had honed their rodeo skills.

She leaned against the railing, studying his profile. "Do you think you'll miss it?" she asked. "If you don't go back to rodeo?"

"I've been giving that a lot of consideration. I liked competing with my brother. Jacob's pretty much been the standard I've always measured myself against. But now that he's a dad, his focus has changed. I doubt he'll be in the arena much."

Did that have anything to do with Daniel not wanting children, the sacrifices and lifestyle changes kids caused?

"The other parts of rodeo that I enjoyed can be duplicated in ranch work," he said. "The horses, the people, the physicality of it. I can't imagine ever sitting behind a desk all day. I like working with my hands, getting sweaty, collapsing into bed bone-tired but satisfied. I guess that doesn't sound sophisticated or ambitious."

"It sounds..." Sexy as hell. "Like you know what you want." But given the comments he'd made about growing up not-quite-a-Baron, she assumed he wasn't planning to do all that sweaty, satisfying work here at the Roughneck. "Did you have a particular ranch in mind?"

"A buddy's helping me set up an interview in Colorado." He straightened suddenly, shaking his head. "I haven't told anyone I'm considering that move. Not even Jacob. I figured I'd hold off discussing it until after Carly's wedding, when I have more details. But you're very easy to talk to."

Adele had told her the same thing on more than one occasion. Nicole acknowledged the compliment with a smile. "Guess it's a skill I cultivated as a kid—getting others to talk about themselves. Took the pressure off me. I didn't like answering questions about my absentee, addict mom. Plus, letting others carry the conversation helped me make friends." Shallow friendships, some of them, with older kids who didn't know Nicole well but liked how important she made them feel. It had helped her survive the constant shifts in households.

"Well, your conversational skills aren't limited to listening," he said, turning to face her. "You did a hell of a job today. You were calm and tactful and respectful of everyone's feelings. Adele couldn't ask for a better ambassador. She's lucky to have you."

She wanted to thank him but had trouble speaking around the sudden lump in her throat. The whole time she'd been talking to the Barons, she'd fought to keep her emotions tightly reined in. The discussion had been awkward enough without a pregnant lady sobbing her way through it. But now that she'd had some distance and wasn't keeping herself so closely guarded, it all bubbled to the surface. How much family meant to her, how desperately she hoped Adele and her children could forge a new relationship, how scared she'd been for her friend during Adele's battle against cancer.

"Hey." Daniel ducked his head, meeting her gaze. "You okay? I didn't mean to upset you."

"I'm fine," she said, trying to sound as if it were perfectly normal to be weepy on the back forty for no apparent reason.

He stepped closer, patting her on the arm. It was an endearingly clumsy gesture, as if he weren't accustomed to offering comfort. She appreciated his making the effort on her behalf.

She grinned up at him. "I really am fine. I've just been worried about how today would go. Repressing all that anxiety finally caught up with me. Sorry if I made you uncomfortable."

"Not at all." He wasn't quite touching her anymore, but he hadn't dropped his arm either. It rested on the wooden railing. "I like spending time with you."

"Same here." They weren't particularly flirtatious or original words, but her tone was deeper, huskier, than she'd intended, making her statement sound like an invitation.

An evening breeze stirred around them. The ends of her hair brushed over his hand, and he caught her ponytail in a light, playful grip.

"We should go back," he said. "It's getting downright chilly out here."

"Is it?" She'd have to take his word for it. Standing this close together, their gazes entwined, all she felt was the tantalizing rush of anticipation.

He leaned in so that his breath fanned against her skin. "Uh-huh." Then he lowered his mouth to hers in a slow, sweet exploratory kiss. His hands, warm and rough, cupped her face as he traced her lips.

Giddy sensation feathered through her. She could barely remember the last time she'd been kissed, much less the last time she'd been kissed with so much finesse. Daniel's kiss wasn't hesitant, merely patient, as if he had all the time in the world to make her feel good. He kept coaxing until the pleasure she was experiencing sharpened into something more insistent.

She boosted herself up on the railing, and his hands went to her hips to steady her.

He deepened the kiss, and thought imploded when his tongue slid against hers. Damn, he was good at this. He stood between her legs, holding her close. Perched atop the railing, she started to hook her feet behind his knees for better balance, but froze, realizing just how intimate their position was. *What am I doing?* She abruptly ducked her head, and he bumped his chin on the top of her skull.

Ow, dammit. "Sorry," she mumbled.

"Maybe I should be the one apologizing." He took a step back but kept his hands on each side of her, not letting her fall. "Did I overstep my bounds, kissing you like that?"

"That was…wonderful." Did she look as dazed as she sounded? She'd be replaying that seductively drawn-out kiss in her mind for a long time to come. "But there's something I should probably tell you before it happens again."

He raised an eyebrow, looking heartened by the idea of an encore. *Unlikely.* Once she made her confession, she didn't think Daniel would be in any hurry to lock lips with her again.

"I'm pregnant."

Chapter Five

Daniel blinked, pretty sure he'd heard wrong. He replayed the words in his head, but every time he tried to process them, he got the same result. "You're what?" He dropped his gaze to her midsection in disbelief. "Seriously?"

She scrambled down from the railing. "No, not seriously. I always make random jokes about carrying a baby after a guy kisses me."

"Right. Stupid question."

Nicole sighed. "It was an understandable expression of surprise. I shouldn't tease you about it. I don't know what the social protocol is here. Maybe I shouldn't have mentioned it. It just seemed like…information you deserved to have."

"Wait. Does that mean there's a guy—"

"No guy. This was a, uh, medical conception." She lifted her chin, a spark of defiance contrasting with the vulnerability in her dark eyes.

"Oh. Good. I mean, good that I wasn't kissing someone else's—" He shook his head, painfully aware that he wasn't handling this with much aplomb. "We really should get you back to the house."

"Yeah." There was a soft note of regret in her voice. "That's what I figured."

Neither of them said much on their return walk, but it was no longer an easy, comfortable silence. He wondered what she was thinking but was afraid to ask. Hell, he wasn't entirely sure what *he* was thinking.

In his defense, the passionate, uninhibited way she'd kissed him back had short-circuited more than a few brain cells. It would be a struggle to come up with responses to even basic statements right now, much less the bombshell *"I'm pregnant."* It was the last thing he'd expected to hear. He'd assumed from Lizzie's pointed looks that Nicole was single, and the shapely brunette sure as hell didn't look as if she was expecting.

Although, hadn't she said something at Lizzie's the other day about her stomach being unsettled? And she'd had her hand across her abdomen when he'd seen her at the—

"That's why you were visiting a doctor," he blurted. "When I ran into you at the medical complex?"

"Yep. I wanted to find an obstetrician here in Dallas since I'll be splitting my time between the two cities until the wind farm is successfully up and running. Plus, we had a management position at the satellite office with Chris's name on it. Since he's no longer with AB and we haven't found the right person to promote, I'll be conducting interviews, too."

Mention of his brother-in-law prompted him to ask, "Do Chris and Lizzie know? That you're, um, pregnant?" Hearing it out of his own mouth made it no less surreal.

"I told Lizzie today when we had a few minutes

alone. So Chris might know by now. It's still very new. I only told Adele a couple of days ago. She was stunned. Maybe not as much as you," Nicole joked. "But pretty close."

"I thought the two of you were like family. You didn't tell her what you were planning to do?"

There was a long pause with only the crunch of their footsteps to break the silence. Finally, she shrugged. "Sometimes, no matter how much you care about them, it's still difficult to talk to family, right?"

She'd just summed up the past twenty years of his life.

"Right."

WHEN NICOLE FIRST got into Daniel's truck to leave the ranch, she was afraid the tension in the cab would be stifling after the hot kiss they'd shared. But it had been a long, draining day. She didn't have enough energy left to be tense.

The radio was set to a country station. During a slow, twangy ballad, she found herself smothering yawns. By the time they reached the apartment building, Daniel had to nudge her awake.

Blinking in the dark cab of the truck, she tried to remember where she was.

Daniel chuckled. "Guess I'm not a very exciting date if I put you to sleep."

And just like that, the evening flooded back in a vivid flash. Her lips tingled as if she were reliving their kiss. "Oh, you were plenty exciting." Any more excitement, and she might have ended up with hay in her hair, searching for her bra. She hadn't had a night like that in recent memory. Then again, she hadn't known many men who could kiss like Daniel Baron. It was hard not to speculate on what would have happened if she hadn't stopped him, if she hadn't told him she was pregnant.

But you are. Her child was her future. Daniel, in the greater scheme of her life, was a momentary diversion. A cowboy who'd been kind to her but would probably barely remember her a year from now.

He parked the car and walked inside with her, automatically aiming toward the elevator banks. She started to tell him that she normally took the stairs, but changed her mind when she realized she was far too tired. The doors parted, and she turned to tell Daniel good-night before entering.

"Thank you for— Oh. You're going up with me?"

"Absolutely. It's late. The gentlemanly course of action would be to walk you to your door." His tone was firm.

She'd been in this elevator with half a dozen people before, yet Daniel seemed to fill the space. There was a larger-than-life quality to him that made her pulse flutter madly. She suddenly regretted ending their kiss so soon. Obviously, they had no future together, but she wished she'd savored the moment longer before it had to end.

"For what it's worth," she said softly, "I had a nice time. Or, as nice a time as possible, under the circumstances. I credit you for that."

"I had a nice time, too." He grinned wryly. "Under the circumstances."

They walked down the hall, and he waited patiently

while she unlocked the apartment door. She paused with her hand on the knob, realizing she'd achieved her goal of making contact with the Barons on Adele's behalf. With that accomplished, they no longer needed Nicole as a go-between. "I don't know if our paths will cross again."

He opened his mouth, clearly on the verge of saying something, then shook his head. "If I ever want to start up a wind farm, I know who to call."

Before she could talk herself out of it, she stretched up on tiptoe, hoping he met her halfway. Otherwise, this would get awkward. "Goodbye, Daniel."

His arms were around her before she finished the words. He gave her a thorough, languorous kiss that made her entire body burn, tracing the seam of her mouth with his tongue and sucking gently at her lower lip. Her earlier thought floated to mind, that he kissed like a man with all the time in the world, but that was a lie. They didn't have time, they had only right now. She'd probably never see him again.

The thought led her to kiss him with increased urgency, tugging him closer to her, imprinting this moment on her memory. When they finally broke apart, her breathing was ragged. And the look he gave her said he was trying his damnedest not to reach for her again.

It seemed pointless to say goodbye again, so she opened the door and stepped inside, knowing it was time for the cowboy to ride away. Granted, he was headed through downtown Dallas, not into a desert sunset, but still…

"How'd it go?" Adele materialized so quickly she must have been listening for the key in the lock. Nicole almost felt guilty for taking the extra time to canoodle in the hallway when her friend was no doubt climbing the walls with curiosity.

"Really well." Pulse still racing, Nicole shoved aside thoughts of Daniel's kisses and tried to refocus on her purpose today. "Carly's particularly anxious to call you. The girls want to come see you soon."

"I'll clear my schedule!" Adele's eyes glistened with happy tears. "And Jet? M-my boy?"

"He…" Nicole faltered, recalling how increasingly somber he'd become while she talked about his mother's depression. "He mentioned not wanting to overwhelm you. He thought you and the girls could use some 'mother-daughter bonding time' first."

"I see."

Nicole laid her hand on Adele's shoulder. "He'll come around. Give him time."

Nodding, Adele smiled sadly. "I owe him that. Frankly, if even one of them forgives me, it's more than I deserve. Thank you so much, dear, for helping me get this far. Now, is there anything I can do for you? Maybe make you a relaxing cup of tea before bed?"

"Thanks, but I'm utterly beat. I'm going to brush my teeth and then collapse." The words felt true when she said them. She was exhausted.

Yet once she snuggled beneath the sheet and blanket, expecting sleep to claim her, she found herself staring at the ceiling. And thinking in great detail about Daniel Baron.

"ARE YOU SURE you want me to be here?" Nicole asked, afraid of intruding on such a personal moment. According to the clock on the microwave, she still had a few minutes to leave the apartment before the Baron sisters arrived for dinner.

"God, yes." Adele clutched her wrist as if it were a lifeline. "Please don't go. They know you. They *like* you. Maybe you can help us revive conversation if we descend into horribly awkward silence."

Nicole chuckled. "I've met Carly. I can't imagine too many silences when she's around." On the whole, Adele's children were a lively bunch. Savannah might be a bit quieter than the others, but she lit up when talking about her store or her husband, Travis.

Adele's smile was bittersweet. "Carly's always been a pistol, even as a toddler."

When the oven timer buzzed, Adele jumped, underscoring how tautly her nerves were strung.

"Why don't you have a seat?" Nicole instructed. "Your blood pressure's probably in the stratosphere."

"I'm the one who should be making dinner. You're a pregnant woman who already put in a full day at the office."

"You did make dinner. The salad's in the fridge, and the rolls are in the basket. All I'm doing is taking your lasagna out of the oven. That doesn't count as heavy lifting." Nicole suspected the real issue was that Adele wanted to stay busy, but there wasn't much left to do. If Adele kept dashing manically about the kitchen, the salad was going to end up on the floor and the glass pitcher of iced tea would end up in shards.

C'mon, Lizzie. From what Nicole knew of her organized, businesslike friend, Lizzie was characteristically punctual. Hopefully that would prove true this evening. If the women didn't arrive soon, Adele was going to work herself into a panic. When the knock sounded at the door, Nicole offered up a silent prayer of gratitude.

She gave Adele an encouraging smile but didn't volunteer to answer the door. This was something her friend needed to do on her own. Adele talked about hoping her children could forgive her, but the truth was, Adele hadn't forgiven herself. She needed to face her daughters, face her past and finally move beyond her mistakes.

Nicole watched discreetly from the kitchen as Adele admitted the trio of Barons into the apartment, the first time in decades all four of them had been in the same room. When they were together like this, their subtle physical similarities became more obvious—how Lizzie's intelligent gaze was so like her mother's or how some of Savannah's mannerisms echoed Adele's.

"Th-thank you for coming." Adele's voice trembled. "I've…missed you all so much."

"Look at you." Savannah sniffled, the concern in her voice unmistakable. "So skinny! I should have brought some of my desserts with me."

"Savannah's quite the cook," Carly said loyally. "And Lizzie's super on top of things. She—"

"You don't have to sell me on how wonderful they are," Adele said. "I already know I have the best daughters in Texas, and that I was a fool to leave you." When tears spilled down her face, Carly and Savannah stepped forward at the same time to hug her. Lizzie hung back a little, but it was clear from her expression that she wasn't unaffected.

Nicole gave them a moment of privacy before stepping out to help greet their dinner guests. She noticed that Lizzie was carrying a large shopping bag.

"I thought I'd show M— Adele the album of Chris and my wedding pictures," she said. "When I mentioned it, Savannah and Carly both had pictures they wanted to bring, too. And, of course, you don't even want to get me started on baby photos. It's like every second of Natalie's life is cuter than the last, and we're determined to document it all."

Nicole grinned. "Well, she *is* a beautiful baby. And I for one would love to see the pictures. They'll give me an idea of all the sweet moments I have to look forward to," she said softly, not sure if Carly and Savannah knew she was expecting. If not, now wasn't the time to tell them. Tonight wasn't about her. "But what if we save the albums until after we eat? The food's hot and ready to serve."

Dinner conversation was halting, at first. As expected, Carly talked about the plans for her upcoming wedding, but the more she expounded on the Big Day, the guiltier Adele looked. She clearly hated that she hadn't been present for either Lizzie's or Savannah's marriage ceremonies.

"Even though she's still really young for the job," Carly said, "we're going to let Luke's little girl, Rosie, be the flower girl. Alex is going to escort her to the front pew, where she'll sit with Luke's mom. We're not going to make her stand through the whole thing. Two-year-olds aren't known for their predictability, and Rosie has her moments. But I'm crazy about her. When Luke and I first started dating, I wasn't sure I was cut out for mother—"

She broke off so suddenly that Nicole wondered if she'd become aware of the mounting tension on her own or if one of her sisters had perhaps jabbed her under the table.

Adele stared at her plate. "Some people definitely make better moms than others."

"I suppose," Lizzie said, "that, in your own way, you were trying to do right by us when you left. Nicole told us your depression was…really bad."

"It was like living in quicksand," Adele said, her eyes haunted, "getting sucked further and further down each day, suffocating. I wouldn't wish that on anyone. I didn't feel fit to be a mother, was afraid that what I was going through would rub off on all of you. Or, worse, that one of you could be hurt through my neglect. Savannah fell one day and when Brock noticed the bruise later, I couldn't even remember it happening. Lizzie, you explained the incident to him, but even hearing it out loud didn't jog my memory. The day remained this horrible gray blank for me. What if it had been a tumble down the stairs, or into the pool?"

Even now, so many years later, Adele looked distraught over the possibility. "I was hurting and I fled. But the very last thing I ever wanted was to cause you girls or your brother pain."

Silence reigned at the table. Then Carly blurted, "Come to my wedding." All eyes turned to her, surprise on more than one face at the non sequitur.

Carly squirmed in her seat. "I mentioned Tammy

being there, but I don't want just the mother of the groom. The mother of the bride should be there, too."

"Oh, I'd love to! If you're sure it won't cause too many problems..."

Lizzie and Savannah exchanged apprehensive looks. Had anyone told Brock that they were meeting with their mother? He'd been pleasant enough to Nicole when she'd been at the ranch, but she imagined he was quite different when he was angry. And he might not appreciate the ex-wife who'd abandoned her family unexpectedly attending his daughter's wedding.

After a moment's hesitation, Carly admitted, "There may be some...awkwardness. But don't most large family gatherings have a little bit of that? To be honest, Daddy doesn't know we're here now. He knows we were looking for you, though. And it's my wedding. I can invite whomever I want. If he knows what's good for him, he won't make a scene that ruins my big day."

"I see." Adele processed that information. "I appreciate the invitation, more than I can say, but the last thing I want to do is cause more trouble for any of you. Talk to your father first. Then, if you're still sure you want me there—"

"Before we can broach the subject of you with Daddy," Lizzie interrupted, "there's something we have to ask you about first. The Baron Energies stock purchases."

As Adele explained she'd bought stocks when prices were low in the spring to help build trusts for her grandchildren, Nicole began clearing dishes. She tried to make herself scarce when Adele and the girls settled in the living room and began looking at pictures, which included a few shots of Savannah's impromptu wedding and Carly trying her hand at bull riding. She was surprised when Lizzie joined her in the kitchen, where Nicole was making coffee.

"If you'd rather be out there," Nicole said, gesturing with her chin, "I've got this covered."

"I know. But I wanted to check on you. Has the morning sickness let up at all?"

"Hard to say. Some mornings, I feel just fine, but then a wave of nausea will hit me with no warning later in the day. I've noticed that stress and not eating anything make it worse." It was counterintuitive—when her stomach was feeling particularly turbulent, her instinct was to avoid eating. Yet more often than not, food could help settle her tummy. "Do your sisters know I'm pregnant?"

"The only person I told was Chris. When I first found out I was having a baby, I didn't want anyone to know immediately. I kept it a secret at work for as long as I could. I understand needing time to adjust—although, I guess, in your case, you weren't caught by surprise." Lizzie gave her a lopsided smile. "Since you planned it."

"The funny thing is, I *was* surprised," Nicole said. "They're constantly refining the process, but having the procedure is no guarantee that it will work." Percentage-wise, the odds had actually been against her. The doctor had prescribed fertility drugs to her beforehand to increase the chances of successful conception. Repeated attempts would have quickly sapped her savings. "I think maybe I was too afraid to get my hopes up. When I saw the positive sign, I couldn't believe I'd been lucky enough for it to work on the first try!"

She wanted this baby so much. She just hoped she could be every bit the mother he or she deserved. "I did tell someone besides you about the baby on Sunday," she said. "I confided in Daniel."

"Really?" Lizzie's eyes widened. "You made it sound as if the two of you were only casual acquaintances."

Nicole reached in the refrigerator and pulled out flavored creamer and an open carton of half-and-half. She was happy to have somewhere to look besides at Lizzie while confessing what had transpired between her and Daniel. "Well…after he kissed me, my pregnancy seemed like pertinent information." They'd been getting along so well Sunday night that he might have asked her out if she hadn't told him. Then what? That would have made for a very awkward conversation three months down the road. Her cheeks heated at the fanciful thought. It had been only a couple of kisses; that didn't necessarily translate to lasting relationships.

Lizzie clapped her hands together. "Aha! I knew the spark I saw between the two of you wasn't my imagination. You like him."

"Yeah, but that's a moot point. I live in San Antonio and am getting ready to have a baby. He…" *Is planning to move to Colorado.* She kept that to herself, remembering he wasn't ready to tell his siblings yet. "Doesn't want a family."

"He doesn't?" Lizzie frowned as if this were news to her.

"I'm sure he loves Natalie," Nicole rushed to reassure her. "I just don't think he sees himself as father material."

"There are times I'm not sure he sees himself as brother material. He can be distant. It's too bad you aren't interested in dating him. When he was around you on Sunday, he was more open. More engaged with the rest of us."

Because he'd been looking out for Nicole, helping her navigate a difficult conversation with the others. She was touched anew by his thoughtfulness. "He's a great guy. And a great kisser. Oops—you probably don't want to hear that." She sighed. "Were your hormones all over the map when you were pregnant? Not just the mood swings or getting weepy, but… Never mind. I don't want to pry, or skeeve you out by lusting after your stepbrother. But if I were a different person, it would be so tempting to indulge in a fling."

Once the baby was born, heaven knew when she'd have time to herself. It could be a long damn time before a man made her feel as Daniel had. Would she regret the missed opportunity? She wasn't sure, but this was a terrible time to ponder that question. Here she was sounding as if she wanted to use Lizzie's brother for sex.

Pressing a palm to her forehead, Nicole muttered, "Lord knows what you must think of me right now."

Lizzie surprised her with a peal of laughter. "Honey, the night I met Chris, I picked him up in a bar for a one-night stand." At Nicole's double take, she added, "Long story."

One with a fairy-tale ending, judging by how happy

she and Chris made each other. But Nicole knew from experience, happily-ever-afters were far rarer than storybooks would lead one to believe.

Chapter Six

Daniel stepped out of his truck and into a brisk gust of wind that sliced through his T-shirt and the lightweight athletic pants he'd chosen for PT. No matter. If today's workout was anything like the last, he'd be warmed up and sweating shortly. He welcomed the hard work and inevitable pain. At least it would help distract him from—

Nicole?

When he first glimpsed the brunette slouched on the bench with her face in her hands, he wasn't surprised by the thought that she looked like Nicole. He'd been thinking about her so much since they'd kissed goodbye a few days ago that he was beginning to imagine resemblances between her and others. The waitress who'd brought him fajitas last night reminded him of Nicole. His mail carrier looked slightly like Nicole. His buddy's golden retriever had big brown eyes that made him think of Nicole. But, apparent mental breakdown aside, the woman seated a few yards away really *did* look like Nicole.

Then she confirmed it by lowering her hands. She wasn't crying, but there was a forlorn blankness in her gaze as she stared straight ahead. She hadn't seen him yet. Actually, she didn't seem to see anything.

He took an involuntary step toward her before remembering he was already a few minutes late for therapy. He found Sierra's number in his contact list and waited while the phone rang. "Hey, this is Daniel Baron. I just wanted to give you a heads-up that I'm stuck in traffic. I'm not far away, but—"

"I'll say. I can see you through the window in the reception area, lunkhead. Is that a woman out there with you? I hope you're not blowing off physical therapy to hit on someone, 'cause I gotta tell you, your sex life would benefit from increased flexibility and strength. Women dig a full range of motion."

"No, I'm not hitting on…" As he got closer, he saw that Nicole looked seriously upset. "Sierra, I need to cancel my appointment. Can we reschedule for tomorrow?"

"I'll check the calendar, but considering the late notice, you're still getting charged for today's session."

"Noted."

"Is she worth incurring my wrath?"

"Yeah." He didn't have to think twice about the answer. "She is."

Finally, he was close enough that the sound of his voice registered with Nicole. She whipped her head around, eyes huge in her pale face. He disconnected his call, silently apologizing to Sierra. He'd make it up to her later. This was clearly an emergency.

"Nicole? What's wrong?" Horrible possibilities loomed large in his imagination. "Is everything all right with the baby?"

An odd, strangled noise emerged from her throat. It took him a moment to realize she was laughing.

"Not *baby*." She made the noise again, an unsettling bark of hysterical amusement. "Bab*ies*."

"What?"

"I just had m-my ultrasound." Her bottom lip quivered, and her eyes shone with tears about to spill over. "And the doc-doctor informed me I'm having…I'm having *twins*. He actually joked about my getting t-two for the price of one!"

After that, it was all sobs. If there were words lost in the flood, he couldn't decipher them. Daniel sat next to her with zero idea of how to respond. He didn't want to say anything that would make it worse. So he put his arm around her in a kind of sideways hug that was meant to be friendly without echoing the more intimate embraces they'd already shared.

She turned into his shoulder, and soon the material of his T-shirt clung damply to his skin. Stifling a shiver, he wondered if she'd even noticed it was cold today. How long had she been out here? Her hands were like icicles. The blouse she wore with her slacks was long-sleeved, but she didn't have on a jacket.

"Nicole? How about we go sit in my truck and talk this over, okay?"

When she nodded numbly, letting him lead her without seeming to care where they were going, he decided he might need reinforcements. He scrolled through the contacts on his phone a second time, this time stopping on Lizzie's home number.

But it was Chris who answered, which seemed unusual for a weekday afternoon. "Hello?"

"Daniel here. Is Lizzie around? I've got a female emergency."

Pause. "Don't you need to be female to have one of those?"

"I'm with Nicole Bennett." Daniel lowered his voice, not wanting to make her feel any more self-conscious. She, however, still seemed to be in her own world. Her crying was now interspersed with hiccups. "She's a little…emotional. I thought another woman, one who's already been through this, might be the right person to talk her off the ledge."

There was another pause. For a second, Daniel thought they'd lost their connection.

"Lizzie *just* fell asleep," Chris said apologetically. "She was up with Nat all night. I called to check on them during my lunch break, and she sounded so wrecked that I came home early so she could take a nap. I swore I could handle everything for a few hours. Sorry. She really needs rest."

Daniel chewed on the inside of his cheek. "Can you ask her to call my cell when she wakes up? In the meantime, I don't suppose *you* have any advice, as the husband of a woman who's been through this?" Lizzie always seemed so composed and in charge that it was difficult to imagine her coming unhinged on a public bench, but if there'd ever been a likely occasion for that, it would have been during her pregnancy.

"If you happen to have any chocolate handy, offer her some," Chris suggested. "You could also try giving her a hug."

"I did that." Sort of. He opened the passenger's door for Nicole and helped her into the truck. Then he said,

"Wish me luck," and hung up as he walked around to the driver's side.

Daniel didn't have any tissues in his truck, but there were some clean napkins from a fast-food drive-through. He handed her those and began rubbing her back as she blew her nose.

"Twins." Her voice was a watery whisper. "I'm having twins."

Clichés sprang to mind about double the happiness, but she didn't need platitudes right now. Besides, he doubted he'd sound very convincing. He wasn't the right guy to try to sell someone on the idea of a bigger family.

For lack of anything helpful to say, he went with the simplest thing that came to mind. "Congratulations?"

She stared at him intently as if she couldn't quite bring him into focus, then snickered a second later. "Way to say it like you mean it, cowboy."

He was relieved by the note of wry humor in her tone. "Didn't mean to sound insincere. But I'm flying blind here, not really sure how to react."

"That makes two of us." Her eyes still glittered, her thick lashes spiky with tears, but she sounded more like herself. She blew her nose again. "I am so sorry. I've tried from an early age to be a low-drama person, not draw attention to myself."

She'd mentioned on Sunday that her birth mother was a drug addict, which probably meant she'd witnessed plenty of unstable behavior. The two situations weren't comparable, though.

He shrugged. "So you had a minor blip in your poise—"

"Minor? I was practically catatonic before you walked up. Lord knows how long I would have sat there."

"It's understandable that you'd need time to process. Hell, I'd freak out over the news that I was having *one* baby, much less two."

"If you were having a baby, the entire medical community would freak out."

"You know what I mean. The idea of having a kid, taking on that responsibility and trying to be a role model, is intimidating as hell." On second thought, pointing out all the challenges she faced probably wasn't helpful. *This is why I needed Lizzie.*

Nicole turned away, staring out the window. "I guess, theoretically, I recognized there was a *possibility* of twins. An increased chance of multiple births is listed as a potential side effect of the meds they gave me, but I never actually thought… Oh, God. I've been telling myself I was prepared for this, but now I feel like I'm free-falling. Two babies, all by myself. What am I going to do?"

"First, you're going to take a deep breath." He hoped it would restore some color to her cheeks. But reminding her to breathe wasn't going to magically dissolve her anxiety.

Inspiration struck. "If you don't mind him knowing you're pregnant, I'll put you in touch with Jet. You remember his fiancée, Jasmine, right?" He'd introduced her to so many Barons and soon-to-be Barons on Sunday that her head was no doubt spinning with names and faces. "As the mother of twins herself, she should have all kinds of practical advice she can give you.

Maybe the two of you can meet for lunch or something."

"Thank you. That would be great."

He took Nicole's hands between his, trying to warm them. "It's going to be okay," he told her. Technically, he didn't have the right to make that promise. How did he know what was in store for her? Yet he had faith in this bright, compassionate woman who'd already survived a lot in her life. "You can do this."

"I can do this," she repeated tentatively.

"Now you're the one who needs to say it like she means it."

"It'll take a few thousand times before I even come close to believing it." She tried to smile, but it was shaky. "I'll practice on my way back to the office."

Back to the office? The last thing he wanted to do was send her off in traffic while she was so distracted by the revelation of twins. "Can't they spare you for a couple of hours?" he asked impulsively. He had some extra clothes in the bed of the truck that he'd planned to change into after therapy, and he was almost certain there was a denim jacket she could borrow. "It's so late in the day already. What's the point in returning now?"

She glanced at the slim gold watch on her wrist. "Holy cow, *that's* the time?"

"You should text someone that you're not feeling well. Play hooky for the rest of the afternoon," he coaxed. "You mentioned needing a Christmas tree. Did you ever find one?"

"No, I didn't get around to looking. It's been a pretty full week."

"Today's one of those days that actually feel like

winter, even in Texas." He always thought it was easier to get in the Christmas spirit when it wasn't seventy-five degrees outside. "What if we went and picked out a tree? I don't have anywhere I have to be." Well, except for physical therapy, but that ship had sailed. He would need to grovel to get back in Sierra's good graces. Still, despite the woman's gruff exterior, he thought she had a bigger heart than she pretended.

"I've never played hooky. I was all about straight *A*s and scholarships."

"Then you have lost time to make up for." He grinned. "C'mon, I'll teach you how to be bad."

STANDING UNDER A tarp where wreaths and refreshments were sold, Nicole sipped her hot cocoa, trying to mask her amusement over Daniel's predicament. He'd been spotted by a boy whose parents had taken him to the rodeo for his tenth birthday, a few weeks before Daniel's injury. Daniel had apparently made quite an impression, and now the boy was talking his ear off. Personally, Nicole hadn't ever spent much time at rodeos, but now she found herself wishing she could have seen Daniel ride.

When he finally broke free of his garrulous young fan, she couldn't help teasing, "I didn't realize I was agreeing to spend the afternoon with a celebrity. Should I be watching in the rearview mirror for paparazzi?"

He rolled his eyes. "You ready to hit another tree lot?"

She nodded, hoping they had better luck at the next place. The trees here, though lovely, had been way too big, impractical for the apartment she and Adele were sharing. Plus, it had dawned on Nicole that she would need to buy decorations. She didn't want to blow her entire holiday budget trying to keep an oversize tree from looking bare. Back home in San Antonio, she had a box of tasteful red and silver ornaments. The end result was a pretty display, but her trees screamed single businesswoman. There were no funky keepsake ornaments with sentimental value or miniature picture frames. She looked forward to adding personality to future Christmas trees, to making homemade decorations with her child—

Children. When would it start to seem real and not like some weird pregnancy dream she was having? From the time they'd left the medical complex, there had been moments when Daniel made her laugh and she temporarily forgot she was the mother of twins; then it would sneak up on her all over again.

"Uh-oh." Daniel shot her a questioning glance as they crossed the parking lot. "You got quiet. At least when you're mocking me, I know you're okay."

"I don't know what I am," she said honestly. "Overwhelmed, mostly. There's a part of me that's excited. I've always wanted family, and now I'm having *two* babies. But on the other hand? I'm having *two* babies!" Panic tried to once again claw its way through her.

Alone at the doctor's office, she'd fallen victim to that urge. But she wasn't alone now. With Daniel's steady gaze locked on hers, she inhaled and exhaled in slow deliberation, recalling how certain he'd sounded when he told her *"You can do this."* She was immeasurably grateful he'd been there today.

"You're like a guardian angel," she told him as he opened her truck door for her.

"Hardly." His lips twisted in a guilty scowl. "A lot of the thoughts I've had near you haven't been very angelic."

His words were like champagne in her veins, fizzy and potent, filling her with a bubbly, lighthearted joy. She hadn't expected him to flirt with her now that he knew she was pregnant. His ability to make her feel so desirable, today of all days, was a minor miracle.

Instead of climbing into the truck, she stopped, enjoying the proximity to him. "If it makes you feel better, I've had some pretty devilish thoughts myself."

He made a low, nearly inaudible sound in his throat, and his gaze dropped to her mouth.

Heat spiraled through her. When they'd said their goodbyes Sunday night, she'd kissed him for all she was worth, thinking it was their only opportunity. But here he was now, within easy reach. *And what is your plan, exactly? To throw yourself at him in the parking lot of a Christmas tree farm?*

With a sigh, she got into the cab. As he started the truck, she finished her hot chocolate. The cocoa was sweet and rich and warm and absolutely no substitute for Daniel's kisses.

As she walked between the rows of Christmas trees, the air fragrant with pine and crisp with cold, Nicole was grateful for the coat Daniel had loaned her. Of course, it swallowed her whole. She often wore high heels at work to make herself more imposing, but the truth was, she wasn't a very big person. *Give it a few months. You will be.*

She actually looked forward to being visibly pregnant; it would make her condition feel more like impending motherhood and not just an erratic case of stomach flu. But, knowing that the physical changes were coming, she appreciated Daniel's admiring gazes even more.

"Hey," he called from around the other side of a Virginia pine, "you're doing it again! Didn't I tell you it makes me uneasy when you get too quiet?"

She nibbled at her bottom lip, not wanting to share that she'd been thinking about all the weight she was going to gain. Instead, she reached out and brushed a hand over the short, twisted pine needles. "We're working to find me a tree, but what about you? Do you already have one at your house?"

"Nah. I have a wreath I put on the door, but I don't usually bother doing much else. Julieta will find a massive tree, and everyone will go over to the ranch to help decorate it. That's where we have Christmas morning, at the Roughneck. Probably the only reason she and Brock haven't taken Alex to find a tree yet this year is because Julieta's been preoccupied helping Carly with wedding plans."

"Well, I love Christmas trees," Nicole said. "During December, I turn on the lights first thing in the morning, so I can enjoy them with my coffee. And I like having them on in the evening. Makes my place less…" She stopped when she realized the adjective she'd been about to use was *lonely*. She didn't want to make herself sound pathetic. She cleared her throat. "Anyway, you might be surprised at what a little Christmas cheer can do for your home."

"It doesn't feel like cheer to me," he said softly. "Not without my mom around."

Her heart constricted in sympathy, and she regretted pushing him to get a tree.

Judging by his faraway expression, he was remembering holidays past. "Mom really got into Christmas. Generally speaking, she was a pretty no-nonsense person. Weathering my father's trial couldn't have been easy for her, but she was tough. And she was tough on me and Jacob, too, grounding us if we got busted for fighting after kids teased us about having a dad who was a crook. She insisted bad behavior was no excuse for more bad behavior. When she married Brock, she had to be firm to run a house with six kids. But at Christmas…

"She did holiday baking and let us eat way more sweets than any other time of the year, including Halloween. Every time she came home from shopping, she'd have a twinkle in her eye and it was obvious she'd found a new gift for one of us." He shook his head abruptly, as if he could rid himself of the memories like a dog shaking off water. "What about you? Did you get to spend many Christmases with your real mother?"

"No. Holidays are a prime time for junkies—way too many excuses to party. They justify that they're being social, that they'll quit after the New Year. December memories of my mother mostly involve her being strung out."

"I'm sorry. I shouldn't have asked."

She reached out and touched his arm. "I don't mind."

Specifically, she didn't mind because it was him. She found herself wanting to share more with Daniel than she did with most people. Perhaps because his own childhood hadn't been textbook "normal" either. Or, perhaps because, even after such a short time, he meant something to her.

"Besides," she added, briefly raising a hand to her stomach, "I have lots of Christmases ahead of me. My babies and I will make new memories."

"Hey!" He grinned proudly. "You said babies, plural, without all the blood draining from your face. That's significant progress."

Maybe not *significant,* but it was a start. She was making progress on the tree hunt, as well. By the time they reached the last row, she'd narrowed her choices to a couple of small but robust pines. Once she made her decision, a man in overalls and gloves helped Daniel secure the tree in the back of the truck while she paid for the tree and an accompanying stand.

As they drove away from the lot, Nicole felt a little pang of disappointment that their errand had ended. Along with a not-so-little pang of hunger. She'd missed lunch. "Daniel, would you have dinner with me? My treat. I want to thank you for going to so much trouble for me today."

"If I agree to have dinner with you, it will be because I enjoy your company," he said. "No other reason."

"Is that a yes, then?"

He nodded. "But I'm not letting you pick up the bill." His lips quirked in a sideways smile. "After all, you've got at least two college educations to save up for."

THE SOUND OF Nicole's laughter filled the cab like music. Daniel found himself exaggerating his funnier adolescent exploits so that he could bask in her amusement on the drive from the restaurant back to the medical compound where they'd left her rental car. He told her about the time during his teen years when he was showing off for one of Savannah's cute friends and accidentally drove the tractor into a tree. Then there was the evening he'd taken his pretty chemistry partner to the barn after studying, supposedly to show her his favorite horse but really in hopes of making out.

Nicole smirked. "Seems like Pretty Girls is the recurring theme in your tales. So what happened when you took her to your barn of iniquity? Because, if the rest of the story is, 'We made out, the end,' I'm going to be seriously disappointed in your narrative skills."

"First, let me remind you, I was fourteen. It's an awkward age for anyone."

"Right, right. I'm sure you've become Mr. Suave in the years since. Get to the good part," she goaded.

"We were almost to the barn, and it was getting dark. Conversation was going well, and I noticed she'd started walking closer and closer to me. In the distance, something howled. Quite possibly a dog reacting to sirens we couldn't hear, but I hinted that it was a coyote."

"Thus scaring her even closer to the big, strong fourteen-year-old?"

"I had decided the time had come to put my arm around her when suddenly an owl—a really big-ass owl—came swooping down in front of us to grab a field mouse or something. I was startled enough to jump. Between being startled and trying to put my arm around her, I…ended up knocking her over. And I may have shrieked. A very manly shriek, though."

Nicole giggled. "So, no make-out session at the barn?"

"She stomped back to the house and later got a new lab partner. I think they ended up going to senior prom together. Meanwhile, I've harbored deep resentment toward owls ever since. If Jacob ever mentions my being 'afraid' of them, it's a vicious lie. I just blame them for breaking my fourteen-year-old heart."

"The entire owl species?" she teased. "Man, you hold a grudge."

"What about you?" he asked.

"You mean do I hold grudges?"

"No." He knew better than that from the wistful way she spoke about her mother. Nicole had been willing to forgive the addict who'd screwed up her childhood. And she believed Adele deserved a second chance, too. Nicole was as kindhearted as she was beautiful. "I meant, do you have any mortifying adolescent fiascos you'd like to share?"

"Oh, look, we've reached our destination. What a shame!"

Since the doctors' offices in the complex all closed by 5:00 p.m., not much expense had been put into parking lights. The poles at the far ends of the empty lot provided only minimal illumination.

She eyed the shadowed crevices between buildings. "This place is creepy at night. But on the plus side, you can see a lot of stars."

"This is nothing," he scoffed. When you'd been raised on a ranch, it was hard to be impressed by a city sky. "You should check out the view from my back porch." It was a casual statement, but as soon as he heard it aloud, he realized how much he wanted Nicole to see that view. He wanted her to come to his house, wanted more time alone with her.

Bad idea. In a couple of weeks, they were each headed their separate ways to very different lives. With the pregnancy, she was already on an emotional roller coaster and didn't need him adding to it. Still, he wouldn't have traded this evening for anything.

When he opened his door, she looked surprised. "You parked right next to my car. I probably don't need the safety escort." But he thought she sounded pleased, anyway.

They'd already decided that from here he would follow her to the apartment so he could help her get the Christmas tree in the building. It wasn't quite a five-footer. Even with his recovering shoulder, he could manage the weight, and he had no intention of letting a pregnant woman carry it.

"I'll call Adele on the way," Nicole said, "so we don't startle her when we come in."

"Do you think she's worried about you?" he asked, knowing she'd left the older woman a vague message about "needing some personal time" this afternoon. She hadn't explained why.

Nicole leaned against her car. "Probably. When she was sick, I worried about her twenty-four/seven. That's what family does."

Exactly. And the bigger the family, the bigger the anxieties. In the past year alone, he'd received calls that Lizzie and Brock were in the hospital and that little

Cody had been taken to the E.R. Between his father going to jail and his mother dying, his childhood had taught him that bad things happen. The more people you cared about, the more risks you took of watching them suffer.

It hadn't cost him anything to look after Nicole this afternoon because she wasn't a permanent fixture in his life. Months from now when she went into labor, he wouldn't have to drive her to the dreaded hospital, wouldn't have to stress over every contraction and complication. When he'd told her he thought she could manage twins, he hadn't been lying. She seemed to have the grit and resilience for it. But parenting was an endless source of fear. Personally, he wanted no part of that.

Nicole's smooth palm against his cheek jolted him from his reverie. "Now who's the one getting quiet?" she murmured. "You look deep in thought."

He tried to joke away his encroaching melancholy. "Nah. My thoughts stay in the shallow end. I was just taking a moment to savor a pretty night with a pretty girl. Recurring theme, remember?" Three years after the owl incident, he'd lost his virginity to a college freshman and lost any lingering shyness around women. But a look from Nicole had the power to jumble his thoughts and send his pulse galloping. "I had a good time tonight."

"Me, too. After everything you've done for me today, Lord knows I shouldn't ask you for anything else. I do have a request, though, while we're here alone." Her hand dropped to his shoulder. He wasn't sure which he enjoyed more, the physical contact between them or the husky note of desire in her voice. "Would you…"

Could he really see a blush stain her cheeks in the dark, or was he imagining it? His heart thudded against his ribs. He thought he knew what she wanted, but he craved the words.

"Kiss me," she said.

Yes. But despite every instinct in his body wanting to do exactly that, he didn't. Not yet. "Nicole, you know I'm attracted to you. But you're going back to San Antonio to a life of raising twins. And I have a plane ticket to Colorado the day after Christmas." His friend Bodie had set up the interview and offered to show him around town.

"I only asked for a kiss, cowboy. I didn't suggest we get betrothed." She huffed out an exasperated sigh as her arm fell to her side. "You're right—pretty soon, I *will* be raising twins. I can't wait to meet them both. But until then, while my life is still my own, doesn't that make this the perfect time to indulge in a few selfish temptations?"

Her explanation made total sense. But he recalled her sobs earlier in the day. He didn't want to take advantage of an emotionally fragile state of mind.

"I shouldn't have said anything." She backed away, opening her car door. "Please forget I did."

"Wait. Nicole, you—"

Her bright smile was patently fake. "See you at the apartment." Then she was shooing him aside so she could shut her door.

Dumbass. Since she'd been at the ranch, he'd thought about kissing her, touching her, at least a hundred times. So why had he turned down something he wanted so much? Worse, he'd embarrassed her in the process.

Maybe he hadn't gotten any better with women since he was fourteen, after all.

THE CHRISTMAS TREE was tightly bound in netting and wire, which simplified getting it into the lobby. Daniel carried it on his left side, primarily using his injured right arm to stabilize it. Nicole had gone ahead of him to prop open the door. He tried to gauge whether she was still irritated about what had happened in the parking lot.

Next time a beautiful woman asks you to kiss her, get over yourself. The more he'd thought about his refusal on the drive over here, the more pompous he felt. Had he really been worried that after a few more kisses, Nicole would return to San Antonio brokenhearted, a hollow shell of a woman just because Daniel didn't want long-term commitments? She herself had pointed out that she wasn't looking for something lasting. She'd simply wanted to enjoy her freedom while she still had it.

As they stood side by side waiting for the elevator, he met her gaze in the mirrored door. She immediately glanced away. But then she flashed another too-bright smile.

"A cowboy, a Christmas tree and a pregnant woman get into an elevator," she chirped. "I feel like there's a joke in that somewhere."

An elderly couple approached just as the doors parted, and the ride up was silent except for the slight jingle of the tree stand Nicole carried in a plastic shopping bag. When Daniel followed her off the elevator, however, he tried to apologize for his earlier reaction. "Nicole, about—"

"Quiet," she cheerfully shushed him. "I'm still trying to think up a punch line."

Despite her doggedly jovial tone, the way she wrenched open the door to the apartment made it clear she was upset. "Adele, I'm home! And I come bearing gifts. Well, one anyway."

A thin, elegant-looking woman who bore little resemblance to the few pictures he'd seen of Delia Baron met them in the entryway. Her gaze went first to Nicole, curious and assessing, as if trying to deduce without explanation the events of her protégée's afternoon. But then she turned her attention to him.

"You must be Daniel Baron." She made this pronouncement with narrowed eyes, as if she didn't quite trust him.

Considering some of the lustful thoughts he'd had about the woman who was like a daughter to her, he didn't blame her. "Nice to meet you. Do you ladies know where you'd like to put this?"

"Here." Adele directed them to a mostly empty corner. The apartment wasn't huge, but neither was the tree, so there should be plenty of space.

Nicole hung back as he and Adele tried to situate the tree in the stand. "I'll let you know when it's straight," she said, directing them to make minor adjustments to the left or right. Adele steadied the tree as Daniel turned the metal screws. He was quiet, trying to decide how to recover from his earlier gaffe. Adele, however, carried the conversation by saying that she'd just ended a phone call with Carly when Nicole and Daniel walked in.

"She's invited both of us to her bridal shower on Saturday," she told Nicole. The happiness on her face when she shared the news made her look twenty years younger. And the sheer enthusiasm in her expression reminded him of Carly.

Nicole appeared less enthused. "Are you sure you don't want the time alone with them? I was planning to work on Saturday to make up for today."

"Please." There was a naked vulnerability in Adele's tone that evoked Daniel's sympathy. It couldn't be easy to face her children after so much time. "The shower's being thrown by Lizzie and one of Carly's long-time friends, Kim. They're having it at the ranch, and I haven't been back there since… Anyway, it wouldn't be time alone. There will be plenty of guests."

"We'll talk about it later," Nicole promised with a wary glance in Daniel's direction. Then she excused herself to get water for the tree. The man at the lot had warned it would need to be watered often for the first few days. He'd also advised against decorating it right away so that the branches had time to "settle" first. Nicole had chuckled at that. Since she didn't actually have any Christmas ornaments in Dallas, waiting wouldn't be a problem.

Daniel felt an almost physical need to hear her laugh, see her smile, again.

"So." Clearing her throat, Adele folded her arms across her chest. "You and Nicole have been spending a lot of time together."

And he'd enjoyed all of it. Would Nicole want to see more of him before she returned to San Antonio, or had he shot himself in the foot?

"We run into each other occasionally because we have doctors in the same office park. Shopping for a Christmas tree was a spontaneous idea." It wasn't his place to tell Adele about the twins or how he'd thought Nicole was too shaken up to drive.

"Do you have any other ideas where she's concerned? Because—"

"Daniel, thank you so much for your help." Nicole reentered the room, sending him a pointed smile. "I didn't mean to eat up so much of your evening. You're free to go now."

He bravely returned her smile. He knew from growing up around females that provoking them came with consequences, but he was unwilling to walk out now with tension between them. "Actually, didn't you say something about one other favor you needed? I wanted to talk to you about that."

Her eyes widened, darting toward Adele. No way did she want him mentioning here that she'd asked him to kiss her. "It's all right," she said tightly. "I've changed my mind."

"I can understand that, but—"

She stepped forward, gripping his elbow. "How about I walk you to the elevator? We can talk on the way." Her eyes flashed, and the look she skewered him with would have made him fear for his safety if he weren't nearly a foot taller than she was.

When they were safely in the hall with the apartment door closed, Nicole whirled on him, socking him lightly in the shoulder. The left one, thankfully.

"What is wrong with you?" she demanded. "It wasn't enough for you to reject me, you had to rub it in?"

He held up his hands in a posture of surrender. "All I wanted was a chance to explain. Not kissing you earlier wasn't rejection. I just— You had a tough day, and I figured you were more vulnerable than usual."

She caught her bottom lip between her teeth, considering his words. "I was only talking about a few kisses in a parking lot, Daniel. That's hardly enough to warrant a *what have I done?* shame spiral later."

"I overthought it," he admitted. "But can you honestly tell me that if we'd exchanged 'a few kisses,' you wouldn't have wanted anything more? Because I can barely stand in an elevator next to you without wanting more." A *lot* more.

Pink filled her cheeks, and she ducked her gaze. "Okay, fair point. I'm a big girl, though. You don't have to worry that if anything happened between us, I'd get the wrong idea. I know we want different things in the long run."

In the long run, they were wholly incompatible. But in the here and now? It sounded as if there was at least one thing they both wanted: each other.

He shifted his weight. "Did I mention the spectacular view of the stars from my back porch? It's supposed to be clear tomorrow night. Can I cook you dinner?"

Her head shot up. "You mean like a date?"

"That's exactly what I mean." A moment passed, and he realized he was holding his breath. He tried to let them both off the hook. "You don't have to answer now. You could call me tomorrow and let me know."

"My answer is yes." Her lips curved in a wicked smile. "But 'spectacular' is a tall order, cowboy. I hope I won't be disappointed."

Chapter Seven

Daniel called Sierra first thing in the morning to apologize for missing his therapy session and to throw himself on her mercy.

"Ha!" she said into the phone. "I don't have any mercy."

Picturing the redhead's slight form, he laughed at her imperious tone. "Has anyone ever accused you of having a Napoleon complex?"

"Not and lived to tell about it."

"I really am sorry I had to cancel last minute. I ran into…" He fumbled, at a loss to describe Nicole and what was happening between the two of them. "A friend who was having a personal emergency."

"I see." Her voice softened. Considering that the therapy building was surrounded by other doctors' offices, there was a wide range of emergency situations that might bring someone to the complex. "Well, I guess that's why I don't have friends," she joked. "I'm never required to worry about anyone but myself."

He knew she was kidding, but, honestly, hadn't she summed up his philosophy pretty well? His own friends were mostly casual rodeo buddies. He preferred a certain buffer of unspoken distance between him and others. Life was less complicated when you didn't have to worry about letting anyone down or dread an inevitable goodbye.

"You think you can squeeze me in today?" he asked.

"No can do, slick. The earliest opening is on Friday. You mentioned that you have access to a heated pool?"

"Yep."

"I'll email you some sheets on low-impact aquatic protocols. Try to do some of those exercises today, and I'll see you at the end of the week."

She didn't know it, but she'd just handed him the perfect opportunity to talk to Anna, the Barons' house-keeper, without being conspicuous about it. He planned to grill a couple of rib eyes tonight, but he wanted to prepare more impressive side dishes for Nicole than a baked potato and bowl of salad. After all, he owed her "spectacular."

Grinning in anticipation of seeing her, he tidied up his cabin. It was a small place, but he hadn't needed much—especially when he'd been on the road so often. The silver lining of living somewhere so compact was that it wasn't difficult to clean. Daniel wasn't a slob; his mother never would have allowed it. He remembered when he'd complained that making his bed every morning was stupid since he was just going to mess it up again at night and had refused on principle. He *also* remembered being grounded for the rest of the week.

Well, his house probably wouldn't pass any white-glove tests, but he thought that if his mom could see it, she'd be reasonably proud of him. Now that he was reminiscing about Peggy, he suddenly wondered what she would think of Nicole if the two women had had a chance to meet. Would she view Nicole as working behind enemy lines, since Nicole was loyal to Brock's first wife? Or would Peggy, who'd briefly been a single mother between divorcing Oscar and her eventual remarriage, commend Nicole for bravely facing motherhood and all it might throw at her?

He got into his truck and made the short drive to the Roughneck, surprised to see both Lizzie's and Jacob's vehicles parked next to the house. He started to knock on the front door but, assuming that Natalie was here with her mom, thought better of it in case the baby was napping. Instead, he slipped in quietly, passing by the closed door of Brock's study. Although Lizzie was on maternity leave until after the new year started, she kept close tabs on what was happening at Baron Energies in her absence. Maybe she, Jacob and Brock were having a management meeting here at the ranch.

Next week, Alex would be out of school for the two-week holiday break, but for now, the house was still. He found Anna in the kitchen, frosting cupcakes at the kitchen island.

"Smells good in here," he greeted her, leaning in to inspect the cupcakes.

She gave him a fond smile. "Thank you, but stay away from those! They're for Alex's class party tomorrow. If you want something sweet, I made a coconut cake the other day. There's probably some left."

"I appreciate the offer, but I'm actually headed out to the pool." He hefted the duffel bag that contained his towel and suit. "I just stopped in to say hi and ask you about recipes. I'm grilling steak tonight and wanted to pick your brain about easy side dishes that are more original than a tossed salad. It must take a combination of genius and magic to get six kids to eat vegetables, but you always managed it."

Her eyebrows inched toward her hairline. "Who did you say you were grilling for?"

"I didn't."

"But it's a girl."

Woman. A hot-blooded, hardheaded woman. And he couldn't wait to see her again.

"Can't I just be looking to expand my cooking repertoire?" he dodged. "I'm not getting any younger, you know. It would do me some good to eat healthier."

Anna snorted. "Is it that Nicole Bennett? The one you brought with you to dinner on Sunday?"

He could once again point out that Lizzie had been the one to invite her, but since he'd definitely issued the invitation for a romantic dinner tonight, it seemed a pointless distinction. "Yes, it's her."

"She's pretty." She lowered her gaze, swirling the silicone spatula in the strawberry frosting. "And she works for Delia. Adele, rather. Is that going to be weird for your brothers and sisters?"

"I doubt it." How much did Anna know about the girls making strides to reconnect with their mom? "Everyone likes Nicole." Not to mention, by this time next month, Daniel might be relocating to Colorado. His dating life wouldn't influence his siblings in the slightest.

For that matter, by this time next month, his social life wouldn't affect Nicole either. She would have returned to her regularly scheduled existence, one that would soon include two babies. Whatever brief time they had, he wanted to make the most of it. She was a special woman. He doubted he'd meet someone who made him feel the way she did anytime soon.

"Well…" Anna spread some icing across a new cupcake. "It doesn't get much simpler than roasted fresh green beans. You could do a cucumber 'ribbon' salad that, when plated properly, looks more elegant and sophisticated than it is. Or I can show you how to make a fruit salad with a pear half that looks like Snoopy's face. Alex is a big fan of that one."

"Thanks, but I think we can skip the Snoopy face." Although…he did love when Nicole laughed. It would be funny to serve her the fruit salad and watch *A Charlie Brown Christmas.*

"When I'm done with the cupcakes, I'll jot down instructions for a couple of quick recipes."

He thanked her again, then went to change into his bathing trunks. The water was warm and welcoming. While the exercises Sierra had sent him were nowhere near as demanding as trying to stay seated on a bucking bronc, he was glad to be doing something physical. Unbidden, Nicole's voice echoed in his head, the note of yearning in her voice when she'd talked about these early months of pregnancy being her last chance *to indulge in a few selfish temptations.* How physical would things get tonight? When she'd drawled her challenge about making their date spectacular, it had been damn near impossible to keep his hands off her. But he'd left without kissing her last night, keeping to his principles. She'd still been processing the news about the twins.

Tonight, however, was about her and Daniel. He'd

give her whatever she wanted. And he'd do his level best to make it spectacular for her.

Daniel was out of the pool and drying off when Jacob emerged on the patio, dressed in slacks and a button-down shirt that was open at the collar.

"You look overdressed for a swim," Daniel said, shrugging into his own shirt. It was definitely too cold outside to be standing around in nothing but wet trunks.

"Anna told me you were out here. How's the shoulder?"

"Improving. But…even after this is all healed up, I'm not sure I'm going to return to rodeo."

Surprise flickered across Jacob's face. "That's a shame. After I came so close this year, I was kind of hoping one of us would make it to the National Finals someday. It would have been awesome to root for you." He hooked his thumbs in the pockets of his slacks. "I know you have some stuff on the side to generate supplementary income, but have you thought about what you want to do full-time?"

"I have feelers out," Daniel said evasively. "You mind if we go inside so I can put on dry clothes?"

"Sorry, didn't mean to hold you up." They turned toward the house. "I came looking for you to see if you're busy tonight. Mariana texted that she'll be late. She's staying after hours for a legal powwow on some big case, so it'll just be me and the little guy. Want to join us for dinner?"

"Actually, tonight's no good. I have plans."

Jacob frowned. "If I didn't know better, I'd say you've been avoiding me lately."

"What are you talking about? I was here on Sunday. And we had beers with Jet after the exhibition."

"Yeah. But even when we're in the same room, it feels like you're not quite present. Or like you're keeping something from me. I know a lot's changed lately, with me juggling Cody and the new job and wedding plans, but I'm your big brother. If something's up, I'm still going to badger you until you tell me what it is."

They'd reached the door to the house, but instead of opening it, Daniel hesitated. "Nothing's up, exactly. I have been thinking about Mom a lot, though. Christmas, you know?"

Jacob nodded. "I'm excited because it's my first holiday with Cody, but even with the excitement… I hate that she never got to meet him."

It went without saying that Jacob didn't plan to introduce Cody to their biological father, even if he did finally make parole. When Oscar Burke had been arrested, he'd been in the midst of running off with another woman, leaving his family behind. He hadn't bothered contacting his sons except once, when he'd thought that, as prestigious Barons, they might be able to help his parole cause.

He should have been released long before now, but he'd been in some fights. The man had a temper. Daniel thought back to some of his own schoolyard fights and wondered if he'd inherited Oscar's angry streak.

"There is one other thing," Daniel said slowly. Jacob had been the most constant member of his family, there for Daniel since the day he was born, and he didn't deserve to be blindsided. "You know how I said I was putting out feelers for job opportunities? Well, some of those opportunities aren't in Texas."

"You're kidding!" Neither of them had ever lived outside Texas. Before moving to Dallas, they'd grown up in Houston. "But…"

"Nothing's definite. Can we keep this between us for now? I thought I'd wait and see if anything pans out then talk to everyone after Carly's wedding."

"I won't say anything," Jacob promised, looking glum. "I can't imagine you not being here, though. I had the mental picture of you helping me teach Cody to ride. Maybe cheering him on in junior rodeo."

"Like Mariana's going to allow junior rodeo," Daniel teased. "Besides, this place is lousy with aunts and uncles for Cody. Jet can help you teach him just as well as I can. You… You're fitting in with all of them a lot better these days. I don't know if it's the job at the family company or being able to relate on the weddings-and-kids front, but I—"

"Don't feel like you fit in? Believe me, I understand. I felt the same way for years. Brock wasn't the most demonstrative dad. At least, not with us. He told me once that he was trying to give us space to get past our anger with Oscar. But when you give the old man a chance, he's not half-bad. Being married to Julieta and having another kid in the house is helping to soften him up, I think. So far he's been a terrific grandfather for Cody."

"Good. Cody deserves that. But since I don't plan to have kids of my own, I'm not too worried about Brock's skills at grandparenting."

"Never say never," Jacob advised. "You think *I* was expecting to be a dad right now? Besides, when you meet someone who makes you feel like I do about Mariana—"

"You don't get it." Daniel didn't *want* that, the mutual obligation and risk that came with falling in love. After years of feeling like an outsider, he'd come to appreciate the freedom that role gave him. He hadn't chafed under the same expectations as Lizzie, the first-born, or Jet, the heir apparent. He'd begun to realize there was a certain kind of emotional safety in solitude.

But that didn't give him the right to torpedo his brother's happiness. "Sorry, I'm cold and cranky. Going in to change now, okay?"

"Sure." But Jacob's tone was subdued.

Daniel felt like a jerk. His brother had been trying to look out for him, just as he always had. "Have you finished your Christmas shopping yet?"

"Are you nuts? I've barely started."

"Maybe you, me and Cody could have dinner out one night and hit a store or something." If Daniel was going to move away, he should make the most of the time he had with Jacob and Cody while he could.

With a start, he realized he'd had the almost identical thought about Nicole. It was odd that he would equate the two. Jacob had been his best friend and childhood hero, arguably the most important person in Daniel's life. How had a woman he'd only known a couple of weeks come to mean so much?

DANIEL FROZE, MESMERIZED by the beautiful woman on the other side of the doorway. "Whoa."

Nicole grinned. "You said this was a date. I don't wear my business suits on dates."

Her loose-fitting, long-sleeved dress was a deep violet with a plunging V-neck that made him forget his own name. The hem stopped just above her knees, and she wore tall leather boots that hugged her shapely legs. Her makeup was minimal and her jewelry was limited to a pair of sparkly stud earrings, but she'd curled her hair so that it tumbled around her shoulders in unrestrained ringlets.

He was probably underdressed in a dark blue henley, jeans and bare feet, but the shirt had been a birthday present from Julieta. She'd said the color brought out his eyes and that women would love it.

He ushered Nicole in and took her jacket, hanging it on the wrought iron rack he kept by the door. "Thanks for making the drive out here," he said. "I know this place is a little off the beaten path." He planned to make her trip worth it.

"It helps that you're not too far from the ranch," she said. "Once I passed that, finding my way here wasn't bad. But I know the drive back to the city isn't short. I have an interview scheduled for tomorrow at eleven and am planning to take the first part of the morning off, in case I...don't get home until late."

"If it's late, you can always crash here," he said casually. "Go back in the morning."

She gave him a lazy half smile. "I'll keep that option in mind."

He filled a couple of wineglasses with chilled sparkling water and asked her how she preferred her steak cooked. He'd seasoned the rib eyes with homemade dry rub and had the meat ready to throw on the indoor grill. Herbed fingerling potatoes were roasting in the oven, and he planned to sauté some spinach with olive oil and shallots. For dessert, he'd stopped in at Savannah's store this afternoon and picked up a pie.

"You inspired me," he told Nicole. "With your talk about how you like to have your Christmas lights on as much as possible so you can enjoy them?"

"Did you change your mind about getting a tree?"

"Nope. But I did put up lights." He pointed upward to draw her attention to the little white twinkle lights he'd strung around the perimeter of the room. He plugged them in, then flipped the switch to kill the overhead light.

She gave him a delighted smile. "It's beautiful."

His phone was docked on a speaker stand, and he pulled up his playlists, inviting her to look for music she liked. He was pleasantly surprised when she settled on an indie band out of Austin that few people had heard of; Daniel knew who they were only because they'd played a set at a regional rodeo over the summer.

"I love them," she said, humming along to an upbeat acoustic song. "One of the guys in our San Antonio office is the drummer's cousin."

"How is the home office surviving both you and Adele being here so long?"

She took a seat at the table and chatted happily about her job, then about her favorite parts of living in San Antonio. It turned out that she, like Daniel, had lived her entire life in Texas. She'd been born in Galveston.

"Texas is home," she said simply. "The great part is that it's so big, home can mean almost anything. Hill country, the coast, forest and wetlands, the panhandle. I can't imagine leaving."

Daniel set a plate in front of her. "I told Jacob today that I was thinking about going. I didn't get into specifics about the interview in Colorado—we didn't have long to talk." Once they'd gone back in the house, there were too many witnesses to the conversation. "But at least now I've let him know it's a possibility."

"Was he surprised?"

"Shocked." He took his seat across from her. "He mentioned that if I moved away, I won't be around much for my nephew, Cody. I've never really thought of myself as role model material. Lizzie and Jacob and Mariana will have that covered. They're all much more organized and driven than I am."

"There are different kinds of role models, Daniel. I didn't enjoy bouncing around foster care, but I did meet lots of interesting people. Some role models teach a kid discipline and perseverance, but it's equally important that someone demonstrates how to nurture your imagination. How to laugh at life when things don't go your way. How to respect nature. I'll bet you'd make a better role model than you give yourself credit for."

He mulled over her words, reconsidering his thoughts today about his inherited temper and getting into trouble as a kid. Maybe instead of focusing on the negative part of his mistakes, he could someday teach his nieces and nephews how to control anger and not let it get the best of you.

"Are you still close to any of your foster families?" he asked.

"Not really. I keep up with some of them—Christmas card newsletters, Facebook, the occasional email. I think when I was younger, I was too hung up on wanting my mom to get clean and come back for me. I resented the people around me, like it was somehow their fault I wasn't where I should be. Eventually, I got old enough to realize how flawed my logic was."

Remembering how sad she'd sounded the day before when discussing her mother's addiction, he changed the subject, asking how Adele had taken the news about Nicole having twins.

"She suspected me of playing a practical joke on her. I had to show her the two heartbeats on the ultrasound before she'd believe me. But in a few months, people might be able to tell just by looking at me. Carrying twins, I'll probably get as big as a house! Most of the pregnancy books say I'm still a couple of weeks away from showing, but I can see it when I look in the mirror. My body's already starting to change."

He couldn't help the reflexive urge to study her body. She didn't look specifically pregnant, but there was a certain delectable fullness to her curves.

She frowned self-consciously. "You're staring."

"I'm *appreciating*," he corrected. "You make me glad to be a man."

This time, she was the one who lowered her gaze in an admiring visual inspection. "You are that." Her breathy tone played along his nerve endings like silk across his skin.

He hoped the food tasted all right, because he honestly couldn't tell. His senses were wholly absorbed with Nicole.

She seemed to enjoy her dinner, though. She ate every bite on her plate. Closing her eyes, she leaned back in her chair with a contented smile. "The music and lighting and perfectly prepared steak… You know how to pamper a girl. I'm not used to anyone cooking for me. I mean, Adele fixes us the occasional waffles in the toaster and she made lasagna when Lizzie and the others came to dinner. But I got so accustomed to taking care of her when she was sick."

"Well, enjoy this while you can," he advised. "When the twins come, you'll be doing plenty of caretaking. Have you adjusted to the idea of having two yet?"

"Hell, no." She grinned. "They'll probably be in kindergarten before it fully sinks in. But I'm doing better than yesterday. Jasmine texted me today about trying to schedule some time to talk. Thank you for that."

"Hey, all I did was connect you to someone who can actually be useful. That's not the same as being helpful myself."

She tilted her head, her smile fading. "Do you really not see how much you have to offer others?"

The question made him feel itchy and restless. "I don't suffer from low self-esteem," he assured her. "You should hear me trash-talk other riders sometime. I'm downright cocky."

That didn't seem to appease her. But after a moment, she sighed. "Never mind. I didn't mean to make you uncomfortable."

When he mentioned the pie he'd bought for dessert, she groaned ruefully. "I don't think I could eat anything else." But she did accept his offer of gourmet minty hot chocolate. They carried two warm mugs onto the back porch, bypassing the small table and padded chairs. They went to the end of the deck for a better view. She hadn't bothered to put her jacket back on, and Daniel seized the excuse to stand close to her, sharing his warmth.

"God. That is amazing." Her voice was a near whisper as she stared at the hundreds of stars twinkling overhead. "I can't believe someone who gets to come home to *this* every night is planning to move. Sorry." She glanced back at him. "I wasn't being critical. At least, not on purpose."

"I knew what you meant. I'm blessed that I get to see this on a regular basis. You should have been here a week ago. There was a meteor shower."

She shot him a flirty smile. "Maybe you should have invited me a week ago."

He took the mug of cocoa from her hand and set it on the railing next to his. "Well, I'm glad you're here now." He slid his fingers through her thick, glossy curls, and she shivered when he brushed the nape of her neck.

"Me, too." She cuddled closer against him, her lips parting in welcome as he captured her mouth in a kiss.

Whether the new year found him moving to Colorado or not, at this precise moment, there was only one place in the world he wanted to be.

Chapter Eight

Nicole was adrift in sensation, almost too much pleasure to process. The rasp of Daniel's fingers against her skin, the sweetness of his peppermint-tinged kisses, the heat of arousal blazing through her. He swept her hair aside, kissing his way down the slope of her neck. His free hand slid past the hollow of her throat, to the curve of her breast. She sucked in a breath, shocked by the intensity of the delicate contact. Her breasts were so excruciatingly, wonderfully sensitive.

At her small gasp, he stopped, pulling away to assess her expression. His gaze sought permission.

She twined her hands behind his neck, bringing him back to her. "When you first kissed me at the ranch, I hated having to walk away from you afterward. I'm not walking away this time."

His mouth found hers again, and their kisses became frantic. He parted the V neckline of her dress with his fingers, sliding the material down her shoulders. The lace cups of her bra gleamed silver in the moonlight. He went still, drinking her in with his eyes as if trying to memorize her.

"So beautiful." Then he palmed one full breast, and

she almost whimpered. She felt ripe and feminine and a little bit primitive, here with him like this beneath the stars.

When he scraped his thumb over one tight nipple, she did cry out. But he absorbed the sound in another searing kiss as he unhooked her bra. She tugged impatiently at his shirt, gratified when they were both bare from the waist up, reveling in the friction of the crisp hair on his chest against her skin.

"Is it too cold for you out here?" he asked, nipping at her earlobe. "We can go inside."

She shook her head, trying to find her voice. When she spoke, the words had a raw, breathless timbre. "You promised me a spectacular time on the back porch, remember?" She could feel his smile against her skin.

"So I did."

Even when he helped her out of her dress, she wasn't chilly. How could she be, when his touch made her burn? He traced a hand down her spine, caressing the small of her back before sliding over the satiny fabric covering her butt. She was so glad they were doing this now and not in another couple of months when maternity panties might be a necessity. His fingers slid beneath the elastic band, driving her mad with his teasing touch.

Well, two could play that game. She reached for the zipper on his jeans, loving the way he gasped when she lightly ran her nails over him. The rest of their clothes didn't last long. By the time she straddled him in one of the deck chairs, she wore only her boots.

In that slow, thorough way of his, he kissed her breasts, making her writhe as need began to outstrip pleasure. She was already on the verge of orgasm when he thrust into her. She rocked against him, almost there, *so close.* Then she threw her head back with a hoarse cry as her climax rippled through her with the force of seismic tremors.

For a moment, their gazes locked, and the expression in his eyes was as hot as the release he'd just given her. Flexing his hips, he moved inside her, hurtling her toward another precipice. And it was spectacular.

A THIN RIBBON of sunlight snuck through the crack between the long curtain panels. Nicole cracked one eye open, taking in the masculine color scheme. The navy curtains, the navy-and-tan-checked comforter. Last night hadn't been a dream. She was really here in Daniel Baron's bedroom, wearing nothing but one of his soft cotton T-shirts.

He was snuggled against her, one hand loosely wound in her hair, the other resting atop her hip. She experienced pure, perfect, bone-deep contentment. Until she tried to move.

The nausea broadsided her like a tsunami, slamming into her so hard that she had an illogical fear of being knocked from the bed. And, since this wasn't her bed, she didn't have any of her usual standbys—the crackers on the nightstand, the acupressure wristbands the doctor had recommended, the trusty bucket she kept on the floor. Just in case.

She groaned as the queasiness roiled through her, praying that if she just stayed perfectly still it would dissipate.

"Nicole?" Daniel mumbled drowsily. If she weren't

focused on not moving a single muscle, she would have smiled at his sleepy tone. The man had expended some serious energy over the past twelve hours. "Did you say something?"

When she didn't answer, he sat bolt upright, inadvertently jostling the bed. She pressed one hand to her stomach and the other to her mouth.

"Nicole, did I hurt you last night?" His voice was urgent now, laced with guilt. "Are you—"

"Morning. Sick." The words took effort, but she couldn't stand the thought of him blaming himself for her misery. He hadn't done anything to her except cause total bliss.

"Oh." The panic in his tone downgraded to sympathetic concern. "What can I do to help?"

Let me die in peace. If she hadn't witnessed what Adele went through with chemo, she might have said the glib words. But she knew that no matter how gut-churningly bad she felt right now, it could be worse.

"Cold washcloth?" she managed. She swallowed hard, closing her eyes against a wave of accompanying dizziness. "M-maybe crackers. And water."

"Washcloth, water, check. I'm not sure I have crackers, though."

"Toast?" she asked weakly, too mortified to reopen her eyes. Last night, she'd been full of heady female power. She'd never felt sexier. But this? This was not sexy. The poor man didn't deserve to wake up next to a moaning, nauseated lump.

"Toast, I can do." He brushed a light kiss to her head, more intention than contact, then stood in slow motion. He must have realized that, to her, his every casual movement was like a hurricane tossing a rowboat about the ocean. "Be right back."

Aware she was fighting a losing battle, she stumble-dashed for the bathroom as soon as he was out of sight. Within a few minutes, the worst of it had ebbed. She pulled a travel toothbrush out of her purse and splashed cold water on her face, hoping to feel human again. But even the return trip to the bed sapped her energy.

On the bright side, it wasn't even eight o'clock. She had plenty of time before she was scheduled to interview a prospective employee at eleven. *Dear Lord, please let me feel better before then.* She wondered if women pregnant with twins got twice as sick as other expectant mothers.

It's okay, guys. She cradled her tummy with her hands. *You're worth it.*

"Wow, there's something I didn't expect to see," Daniel observed from the doorway. "You're smiling."

"I was just talking to the babies." Did the admission sound foolish to him? Oh, well. She'd already blown any chance at a flirtatious, urbane morning after.

"Here." Daniel unrolled a cool, wet cloth across her forehead.

"Thank you. I'm so sorry about this."

"Don't be. It's the circle of life. Or karma, or something. Jacob had to nurse me through my first-ever hangover, which went a lot like this. But, in my case, there was tequila involved."

She shook her head in disbelief. He made her laugh, he cooked, he nursed the ill and he was the best lover she'd ever had. Pretty much the perfect man. Except of course for the pesky drawback of him not wanting kids or a family—the two things she'd desperately wanted since she was a kid herself.

WHEN A 4x4 with tall off-road tires cut into his lane, as if being a bigger truck was synonymous with right-of-way, Daniel let loose a stream of expletives. But he could have just as easily been aiming the words at himself as the other driver. The profanities had been on the tip of his tongue since before Nicole left his place with a hasty goodbye. After she'd taken a few bites of toast earlier, she'd drifted back to sleep, clearly exhausted. He'd wanted to kick himself for the slight shadows beneath her eyes. He should have handled her more gently, maybe stopped after the first—or even second—time they'd made love.

What the hell had he been thinking? *About losing yourself in the most gloriously sexy woman you've ever taken to bed.*

Well, yes. That.

But Nicole wasn't only a sexy woman. She was the pregnant mother of two. He needed to keep that in mind. Unfortunately, when he dwelled on that, anxiety bubbled up within him. She'd chided him for not recognizing what he had to offer, but the truth was, he had nothing concrete or permanent to offer her. He was a temporary distraction, but maybe he'd filled that role too exuberantly.

After she'd fallen back asleep, he'd let her rest as long as he thought he could without screwing up either of their schedules. She had that interview to conduct, and he was supposed to be working with a client in Fort Worth. Daniel had trained an Arabian mare for the man, but he occasionally supervised his client's sessions with the horse to make sure progress was consistent. Also, the client had asked him to be present for today's veterinarian visit.

It was good Daniel had a full afternoon ahead of him. Stewing in guilt and replaying erotic scenes from last night was not a productive way to spend the day. Staying busy would help him forget about Nicole for a little while. Theoretically.

Who are you kidding? The image of her wearing nothing but lace-trimmed lingerie and leather boots in the moonlight? There wasn't enough busy in the world to erase that.

THE INTERVIEW WAS the best Nicole had conducted in weeks. *Because the candidate was truly that wonderful?* she asked herself afterward. *Or are you just in a really good mood today?*

Possibly both, she admitted as she unwrapped a turkey sandwich at her desk. Sure, her day had begun rather inauspiciously, but once her nausea had evaporated, like a dense early morning fog lifting to reveal beautiful sunshine, she'd felt amazing.

She returned a bunch of calls, set up another newspaper interview publicizing the wind farm project and made a respectable dent in her email inbox. One of the emails from a colleague in San Antonio ended with her coworker counting down the hours until tomorrow's opening of a new action movie that starred a mutual favorite actor.

I wonder if Daniel would be interested in seeing it with me. It was hardly the first time today she'd found herself thinking of him, but up until now, she'd avoided wondering when she might see him again. This was uncharted territory for her. She'd never indulged in an affair that she knew had no future. She'd been goal-oriented from a young age, and she didn't like wasting time on anything pointless.

But this didn't feel pointless. It felt more like…a vacation, something exotic and wonderful that you accept from the start is fleeting. Before her reality shifted to midnight feedings and more diapers than she could count, she had these couple of weeks in Dallas with Daniel. He was key to the equation; she didn't know any other man who could have inspired her to behave in such an out-of-character fashion.

So, now what? After assuring him she was an adult who wouldn't get starry-eyed and mistake their time together for a burgeoning relationship, she didn't want to call too soon and seem clingy. Yet, since they were limited to only these couple of weeks, she didn't see the point in playing coy and throwing away time they could have enjoyed together either. It was a relief when her phone rang, reminding her that she was supposed to be a confident executive, not a nervous sophomore fretting over whether or not to ask a boy to the Sadie Hawkins Dance.

"Nicole Bennett speaking."

"Hey. It's Daniel."

Beneath the desk, where she'd kicked off her red patent pumps, her toes curled. "I was just thinking about calling you," she admitted. "You were so great this morning. I wanted to say thanks."

"Are you feeling better now?"

"Completely. It can be intense while it lasts, but once it's over, it's like it never happened." An appropriate metaphor for her affair with Daniel? She tried to ignore that depressing thought.

"How'd the interview go?"

"It was really promising. I have to talk to Adele before I make an offer, but I have a good feeling about the candidate. Finally! I was beginning to despair of ever finding someone who was the right fit. This may call for a celebratory piece of chocolate pie at that bakery Lizzie introduced me to. You're welcome to join me if you're in the area." There, that sounded casual. Message: *I'd be interested in seeing you again, but no pressure.*

"Actually, I have plans tonight. Jacob and I are taking his son Christmas shopping. But *you* could join *me*," he blurted.

For a family outing? She was more confused than ever about the boundaries of this holiday fling.

"It's weird that I invited you, isn't it?" he said, sounding as if he second-guessed himself. "It was a wild impulse. But Jacob and I have three stepsisters to shop for, plus Julieta. A female's opinion could be really helpful, and given your love for Christmas, I thought... I completely understand if you're not up for crowds and a couple of hours on your feet. You, uh, didn't get much sleep last night."

She smiled at the reminder. "Neither did you."

"Totally worth it—even if I was so sleep-deprived that I kept mixing up the horse's name and the client's. I don't think Tony appreciated my calling him Sugarhoof."

"You did not!"

"Okay, I may have exaggerated that part. But I did call the mare Tony."

"Is Sugarhoof really her name?" she asked skeptically.

"You obviously don't attend many rodeos or watch televised races like the Kentucky Derby. Next to some of the more bizarre names out there, Sugarhoof is the nondescript John Smith of the equine world."

She laughed, glad he'd called. Talking to Daniel was better than chocolate pie. "Maybe I will join you guys tonight. If you're sure it will be okay with your brother? After all, Christmas shopping is more fun with company, and I can't go with Adele since most of the gifts I plan to buy are for her."

They agreed to meet in the mall food court. She should have just enough time to swing by the apartment and change first. Her lower back was aching a little bit, and she didn't relish the idea of shopping in the shoes she'd worn to work.

Aches and pains aside, she was looking forward to the evening ahead. During her two recent dinners with Daniel, he'd told her enough stories about his brother that she was starting to feel as if she knew Jacob. He was obviously a terrific guy for his brother to look up to him so much. She wondered if Daniel had considered how difficult it would be to live so far away from the sibling he obviously idolized, but that was none of her business. Maybe she was projecting her own desire for a close-knit family onto someone who would be perfectly happy to keep in touch through online photos and holiday visits.

"Afternoon, stranger."

Nicole glanced up to see a smiling Adele in the doorway. "Hi. You get that text I sent you earlier? If you're available next Monday, the two of us should take that interview candidate to lunch. I think you're really going to like her."

"I did get your text, and I'm glad we have a solid lead. I know you worry about leaving me in the lurch when you go on maternity leave."

"True, but that's still months away."

"Time flies faster than you expect," Adele said wistfully. "But I'm not worried at all. You're the most competent person I've ever hired. I know you'll have everything organized and laid out for us so that your absence causes minimal disruption. And speaking of absences, roomie…" She gave Nicole a pointed look.

Nicole didn't know whether to be amused or exasperated by the warmth flooding her cheeks. *Seriously?* She was almost thirty years old, well past the age of consenting adult. It was ludicrous for her to blush just because she'd stayed out all night. "I did tell you not to wait up for me. You weren't worried, were you?"

"Not in a pacing-the-floors, what-if-she-wrapped-her-car-around-a-tree kind of way, no." Adele stepped farther into the office and shut the door for privacy. "I do worry, though. You know I think the world of you, dear. You're compassionate and sharp and very special. I couldn't be prouder if you were one of my daughters, and I thought it was a crime that you were so busy taking care of me and helping run my company that you didn't have time to date.

"Not that you *need* a man," Adele clarified, "but

marriage and family have always been on your horizon. So I'm tickled that you've met someone who appears dazzled by you. The way he looked at you the other night?" She fanned herself with her hand. "But your situation is unique. If things got serious between the two of you, he'd be committing to an instant family. And even if he *thinks* he might be ready to parent two babies—"

"He doesn't, trust me. And things between the two of us aren't going to get serious."

Adele cocked her head to the side, her expression perplexed. "How could you possibly know that? Emotions aren't always planned or easy to control, the negative ones *or* the positive ones."

Thinking carefully, Nicole tried to find the words that would ease her friend's concerns without diminishing Daniel's worth. He was a hell of a guy. He just wasn't the guy for her. "He and I have talked about our very different future plans. He hasn't shared all of his with his siblings yet, so it's not appropriate for me to tell you about them. But we know we're not looking for the same things. We're just enjoying each other's company, having uncomplicated fun. You don't have to worry that I'm getting too attached."

Adele pursed her lips, her body language dubious.

"I promise." Nicole smiled wryly. "This isn't going to end in me wearing pajamas for a week, listening to sad songs and eating ice cream out of the carton. It's not like that between us."

"All right," Adele conceded. "I shouldn't have poked my nose where it didn't belong. You've always had a good head on your shoulders. No more fussing on my part. Now, if you're about done for the day, how about we go have dinner and you tell me more about this woman you want to hire?"

"Oh. I, um…I'm not actually free tonight. I'm going Christmas shopping. With Daniel," she added, lifting her chin slightly. She'd just explained that she and Daniel enjoyed each other's company. There was no reason to feel self-conscious about running such an innocent errand, especially with his brother and nephew there as chaperones. So why did she feel as guilty as the time she'd knocked over a foster mother's vase and broken it on her first day in a new house?

Adele sighed, then turned on her heel to leave the office.

Nicole exhaled slightly, glad to see her friend had been sincere in her "no more fussing" pledge. "I really expected you to give me grief about seeing him two nights in a row."

"No. I'm not going to say one word about it. But while you're out, dear, you might want to look for some comfy pajamas and stock up on ice cream. Just in case."

Chapter Nine

Daniel was freshly showered and changed into clean clothes when his brother knocked at the front door.

"Ready to go?" Jacob asked. Standing next to him, looking like mini-Jacob, Cody raised his arms. "Hug, hug!"

Daniel scooped the kid into a quick hug, then set him back down. "Ready."

Even after two months, it still made Daniel do a double take to climb into his brother's pickup and see, instead of a bull rope and a bag of rosin tossed on the backseat, a toddler's car seat and plastic toy trucks. The soundtrack had altered, too. Fewer songs about beer and rodeos, more songs highlighting phonics.

When Jacob obligingly hit Repeat on a tune Cody particularly enjoyed, Daniel decided it was as good a time as any to mention his spur-of-the-moment invitation to Nicole. It had been completely unpremeditated. He'd just been so happy to hear her voice and he'd realized he wouldn't see her tonight, or tomorrow evening because of Luke's bachelor party, and then she was attending that bridal shower on Saturday... The words had just spilled out of his mouth. He hoped Jacob wouldn't mind. If there was one thing his brother had demonstrated, it was that he could be flexible and adapt easily to the unexpected.

Daniel cleared his throat. "So, you remember Nicole."

"The pretty brunette you brought to the ranch four days ago? The one you couldn't take your eyes off of?" Jacob teased. "Or are we talking about some other Nicole?"

"She and I have been talking this week." Among other things. "And she has some Christmas shopping to do, so I mentioned we were going to the mall tonight. She's planning to meet us, if that's okay. I, uh, figured she could give us input on gift ideas for the girls."

Jacob snorted with laughter. "You must have it bad if you're using that lame excuse to spend more time with her."

"I don't know what you're talking about. Besides, you have no room to needle me about going out of my way to spend time with a woman. *You* moved Mariana into your house right after you met her!"

"That was to help Cody make the transition, and you know it. But I'm sure as hell not sorry about how everything worked out." Biting his lip, he cast a quick glance at the rearview mirror to see if his son had caught his use of the *H*-word.

"Anyway. You don't mind, do you?" Daniel asked. "Because if you'd rather this just be a guy's night, I could call her…"

"Of course I don't mind. If she's important to you, I'd like the chance to get to know her better. To bond. To warn her that if you're ever in the general proximity of an owl, she should expect to be shoved to the ground while you run off shrieking like a girl."

"I did not run off. And you didn't even witness it happen."

"True. But I've imagined it plenty of times, and in my head it's hilarious."

Daniel rolled his eyes. "One other thing about Nicole…" She'd mentioned that the nausea could come and go suddenly. If it happened to sneak up on her tonight, he didn't want Jacob to think Cody had been exposed to stomach flu. Besides, now that Lizzie, Chris, Jet and Jasmine all knew about the pregnancy, it wasn't much of a secret. She'd said this morning that, between medical appointments and the side effects of carrying twins, she'd need to start telling her coworkers soon.

Lowering his voice just in case Cody had developed an interest in the conversation, he said, "She's pregnant."

"What?" Jacob took his eyes off the road just long enough to gape at Daniel. "But you aren't—"

"Of course not! She decided she was ready to be a mother and was artificially inseminated." Might as well explain the situation now, in case her pregnancy came up tonight, and spare Nicole any awkward questions. "She's most of the way through her first trimester, and she's been keeping it pretty quiet."

"So you're involved with a pregnant woman?" Jacob looked as if he was having difficulty digesting this information. "Because the other day, you said—"

"We're not that involved. Just because the rest of you have all caught wedding fever doesn't mean I'm looking to settle down."

From the backseat, Cody piped, "Hungry! Crackers? Peese," he added dutifully.

Jacob asked Daniel to dig through the bag at his feet and find the animal crackers. In Daniel's limited experience, the crackers wouldn't ruin Cody's appetite for dinner. For a little guy, he could put away an impressive amount of food. It must take a lot of fuel to keep him running at Mach 10, which was Cody's usual speed when not restrained in a car seat.

As Daniel passed a couple of the crackers to his nephew, he reiterated to his brother, "I like Nicole a lot. But that's all it is." Though he'd dated a number of women, he didn't think he'd been in love his entire adult life. Which suited him just fine. Better to leave the long-term entanglements to people who could let themselves be happy without spending all their time waiting for the other boot to drop.

By the time he was a teenager, he'd witnessed adultery, divorce, imprisonment and death. His stepsiblings had dealt with abandonment. Nicole had coped with her birth mother's addiction and Adele's cancer. In the past, Daniel had met people who seemed shocked he would willingly ride bulls for a living. "Isn't that dangerous?" he'd been asked numerous times. Definitely. But as far as he could tell, life in general was a series of treacherous perils.

At least in the rodeo ring, you saw it coming.

NICOLE LEANED AGAINST the metal railing that overlooked the lower level of the mall and watched as Daniel and his brother approached. Many a female head turned to watch them pass. As if the two dark, tall and handsome men weren't attractive enough, Jacob had the added appeal of carrying an adorable toddler. Nicole imagined she could hear the sighs that followed them.

Neither man seemed aware of the interest they drew, probably because they'd had years to get used to it, plus the rodeo experience that helped them ignore onlookers and focus on the task at hand. Still, she couldn't deny that it was heady, the way Daniel seemed too intent on her to notice other women. His gaze had locked on her the second he stepped off the escalator.

She grinned in greeting, wanting to kiss him hello but feeling shy about doing so in front of his brother and nephew. "Hi, there. You guys got here just in time. The smells coming from the food court are so enticing, I was about to give up waiting and go get dinner." She was, after all, eating for three.

"Hungry!" the little boy declared.

Jacob laughed. "So that's two votes in favor of eating right away."

They passed one sit-down restaurant on their way to the horseshoe of casual, to-go vendors that took up half of the second story.

Daniel inhaled deeply. "I see what you mean about the smells getting to you. I was fine until now. Suddenly, I'm famished. Of course, the steak house would take too long. A meal in there would cut too much into our shopping time."

"After last night," Nicole told him, "I won't want steak for a while. What you fixed was so good, everything else is bound to be a letdown." She became belatedly aware that Jacob was watching them, his expression curious.

"Daniel cooked for you?" he asked.

"I suppose you have some smart-alecky remark to make about that?" Daniel grumbled good-naturedly. To Nicole, he said, "He's already hit his quota on giving me grief about owls."

"Nothing smart-alecky. It just reminded me of the first time Mariana came over," Jacob said. "I cooked for her and Cody. She seemed surprised I knew how."

If they didn't stop talking about cooking and food, Nicole's stomach was about to start growling. She scanned the options, trying to decide what she felt like. The place that sold customized salads was probably the healthiest choice.

Meanwhile, Cody had become distracted from his quest for food. He was pointing at the small carousel tucked in the corner by an ice-cream parlor. "Migo!"

Jacob laughed. "We've been over this, buddy. Not all horses are Amigo, and not all doggies are Buster. Our pets," he told Nicole. "Cody loves animals."

The casual comment made her wonder about her own children, what their likes and dislikes would be, whether they'd have mutual interests or be total opposites. It was exciting to imagine getting to know them and watching their personalities develop. At moments like this, she blocked out the anxiety about everything she needed to do to get ready and couldn't wait for them to be born.

When she realized she was absently rubbing her stomach—and that Jacob had noticed—she asked, "Did Daniel tell you I was expecting?"

He nodded. "Congratulations. I missed Cody's early months, so I'm no authority on infants, but I can tell you, there's no feeling in the world like looking down into that little face and being overwhelmed by love. Six months ago, I didn't know he existed, and now there's nothing I wouldn't do for him."

A lump rose in her throat. She blinked, determined not to do something as undignified as start blubbering in front of a place that sold chicken-fried ears of corn and barbecued sausage on a stick.

"Good grief, Jacob." Daniel inserted himself between them, scowling in mock aggravation. "We haven't been here five minutes, and you've already made her cry. Nice going." He waved Jacob and Cody toward the pizza counter the little boy had been eyeing at the other end of the corridor.

Once father and son had walked away, Daniel turned to her with an impish smile. "I thought they'd never leave." Then he pulled her to him for a brief but ardent kiss. He pressed his forehead to hers. "I've been wanting to do that since I saw you from the bottom of the escalator."

She grinned. "You must've been reading my mind, then."

"Do you know what you want?" He winked at her. "Food-wise, I mean."

Hand in hand, they walked to the salad place, then rejoined Jacob and Cody at an empty table.

As they ate, Jacob entertained her with stories of trying to baby-proof his home. "Mariana might be able to give you some pointers on that and other stuff." He ruffled his son's hair. "She was part of Cody's life from day one."

She shook her head wryly. "Between seeking advice

from Jet and Jasmine on raising twins— Oh, Daniel didn't mention I'm having twins?" She laughed at Jacob's expression. "Anyway, talking to you and Mariana, Jet and Jasmine… This must be what they mean by 'it takes a village.'"

Jacob nodded. "I know I'm grateful I have people around me I can ask for tips. And favors. Cody's only been in my life for a couple of months, but we've already had a few babysitting emergencies. This would be impossible without support." He grimaced, as if suddenly recalling she didn't have an extensive family network.

She appreciated the Baron siblings' willingness to offer encouragement and guidance, but she should be careful not to rely too much on others. They weren't *her* village, they were Daniel's. Only, he didn't want them.

After they finished their food and cleaned up the table, they hit a couple of stores. Nicole offered her opinion on a pretty scarf for Julieta. They "cheated" picking out presents for Carly and Luke by using the couple's department store registry to select gifts for both Christmas and the wedding.

As they waited for the clerk to hand over the receipt, Jacob asked, "So will you be coming to the wedding with Daniel?"

"I…" She faltered, not sure of the answer. They hadn't discussed it. She'd been expressly invited to the bridal shower Saturday, but not the ceremony itself.

But Daniel met her gaze, looking untroubled by his brother's question. "Sounds like a great idea to me. I look forward to watching you do the Chicken Dance at the reception. What do you say, be my date to Carly's wedding?"

Warmth bloomed inside her at the easy way he'd included her, his repeated demonstrations that he wanted her company. "Yes to the wedding. A firm don't-get-your-hopes-up to the Chicken Dance."

They exited the department store, and, as they returned to the congested center of the mall, she caught a glimpse of Jacob's profile. Was it her imagination, or did he look smug? Maybe Lizzie wasn't the only one who'd thought matchmaking between Nicole and Daniel was a good idea. She smothered a sigh. She could have told them that she and Daniel didn't need help being pushed together. Mutual attraction was not a problem.

Cody began wiggling with excitement, chanting "Santa!" Sure enough, there was a North Pole display a few yards away. Despite the overall crowd, the line to see Mr. Claus wasn't too long.

"You two mind if we humor him?" Jacob asked. "Mariana and I already took him to get his official picture taken, but…" He broke off, his eyes twinkling. It was clear he was enjoying his first yuletide season with his son.

"Fine by me," Nicole said.

They got in line behind a couple with three kids. The youngest, cradled in her mother's arms, looked only a few months old and was completely adorable in a tiny red velvet dress. The woman passed the baby to the father so she could lean down and fix her preschooler's hair. Nicole's eyes stung. She couldn't honestly say whether she was reacting to the miniature perfection of the infant or the fact that the mom had a partner to share these small, everyday moments.

Irritation welled within her. It wasn't as if she'd made the decision to be a single mom lightly. She'd known what she was getting into, so why did the idea now cause her these periodic twinges of sorrow?

"Nic—" Daniel's questioning tone broke off as he followed her gaze. If he'd been about to ask what was wrong, he'd answered his own question. He shook his head. "Are you going to get misty every time you see a cute kid for the next six months?"

Quite possibly. She shrugged.

"Hey, you think something over there might work for Lizzie?" He pointed past Nicole's shoulder at a window display for a store that specialized in business gifts—briefcases, high-quality pens and coffee travel mugs that could be monogramed or engraved. "Will you come look with me?"

"Sure." She let herself be dragged away since, ostensibly, giving her expert opinion was one of the reasons she was here. But she couldn't help question the pattern. Upstairs, he'd run off Jacob when he and Nicole had been bonding over the emotional rewards of a child's love. And now he was leading her away from the cute baby.

Was he discomfited by her getting sentimental over parenthood? Did he dislike the reminders that her own babies were on the way? That possibility rankled but, really, why should it matter? He'd be long gone before her own children were ever born. Which, somehow, didn't make her feel any better.

"ONE FINAL STORE?" Jacob asked, looking to Nicole and Daniel for input.

Daniel glanced down at his nephew. "I can make it. Not sure about him, though." The last time Daniel had seen eyelids that heavy was on a cartoon dog.

Nicole offered a murmur of assent but didn't say anything. Come to think of it, she hadn't said much for the past fifteen or twenty minutes. Daniel shot her a questioning glance, but she didn't meet his gaze.

"This is the place that's supposed to have top-of-the-line coffeemakers on sale. Mariana wants me to get one for her mom." Jacob scooped up his son, and by the time a salesclerk had shown them to the right aisle, Cody was snoring softly against his dad's shoulder.

Jacob turned to Daniel. "Can you take him a minute? I need to compare a couple of these boxes. I should have picked up Lucille's gift sooner—we're leaving for Austin Monday after work—but with the new job and best-man duties, time's been flying."

Jacob and Mariana were having an early Christmas with her mom and grandmother in Austin and would return for Christmas Day with the rest of the Barons. Daniel knew his brother wanted to make up for Thanksgiving, when he and Mariana had been briefly separated, casting a dark cloud over the holiday. But that was behind them now. This Christmas would be their first as a family.

"Here." Daniel held out his arms. "I've got him." The sleeping toddler weighed less than saddles Daniel had lifted; still, he was careful to nestle the boy against his uninjured left side.

Once he had Cody situated, he looked up to find

Nicole watching him. Was it fatigue or sadness that haunted her eyes? The pregnancy mood swings made her difficult to read. It was sometimes tough to distinguish whether he'd done something wrong or if she was reacting profoundly to something that might not have bothered her on another day.

"You okay?" he asked.

"Of course not." She gave him a wan smile. "I'm counting the days until I can have caffeinated coffee again. I'm not a morning person, even when the mornings get off to a smoother start than today's."

They waited at the front of the store while Jacob paid for the chosen coffee machine. Nicole nodded to Cody. "He looks like you."

"Well…he looks like his daddy. Jacob and I have always shared a strong resemblance." It was a silly technicality to argue. But it was important she didn't convince herself she saw something that wasn't really there.

When Jacob emerged, Daniel happily swapped Cody for the large shopping bag. They'd all parked near the food court. Daniel walked Nicole to her car while Jacob buckled Cody into his car seat.

"I'm glad you came with us," he told her, wondering if she felt the same. She'd been teary at least three times and had become uncharacteristically withdrawn over the past half hour.

In response, she flashed him a smile. It didn't reach her eyes.

When she pressed a perfunctory kiss against his cheek and darted into her car, seeming eager to part ways, he had his answer about whether she was upset or simply tired.

"Nicole..." Part of him felt as if he owed her an apology. But what had he actually done wrong?

She gave him another one of those not-quite smiles. "It's getting late, and I don't want Adele to worry about me. Better get home before I turn into a pumpkin."

He straightened so she could shut her door, frowning at her fairy-tale reference. In some ways, she resembled a fairy-tale character—brave and resourceful, overcoming misfortunes in her quest for happiness. Too bad Daniel wasn't cut out to be anyone's happy ending.

THE BLONDE DEALER on the other side of the table flashed a contrite smile as she flipped over the ace of spades that gave her blackjack. Meanwhile, Daniel's cards added up to seventeen points. *Not my lucky night.*

When he got up to give someone else his spot, he discreetly checked the time. Out of deference to Luke, the guest of honor, and Jacob, who'd arranged the evening, he didn't want to broadcast his desire to leave. Although Daniel enjoyed an occasional game of poker, this glitzy private party in a Dallas hotel wasn't his idea of a good time. Bass-heavy remixes of Vegas standards vibrated the room, the cocktails all had ridiculous novelty names, and one of Luke's cousins responded to everything from joke punch lines to decent card hands with a shrill "Wooo!" that could probably be heard all the way to the front desk.

Someone bumped Daniel and he turned, realizing it hadn't been an accidental collision. Jacob was nudging him to get his attention over the music.

His big brother peered at him. "You do know we're only playing for chips and door prizes, not actual money right? Because you look as miserable as a man who genuinely lost his fortune."

"Just trying to add some casino realism."

"You also look like a guy who's thinking about sneaking away," Jacob said knowingly. "Plans with Nicole?"

Hardly. Daniel shook his head, wishing he did have plans with her. They hadn't spoken all day. He'd stared at her number on his phone half a dozen times but opted to give her space.

He rubbed his arm. "I think maybe I overdid it in physical therapy this morning. My shoulder's killing me. You reckon anyone would miss me if I ducked out early?"

Jacob hesitated, as if trying to decide how to respond. His expression was incongruently somber for someone celebrating at a bachelor party. Behind them, another exuberant *"Wooo!"* resounded.

Get me out of here.

Finally, Jacob said, "Yeah, you'll be missed. But I don't want to stop you from going if that's what you need to do."

"Brotherly powwow?" Jet appeared suddenly, edging between them and draping one arm around each of them.

"Nothing major," Jacob said. "Daniel was just saying good-night."

"Already?" Jet dropped his arm and pointed across the room. "I was going to see if either of you wanted to try your luck with me at the roulette table. I am on fire tonight! Too bad we're not gambling actual cash, or I'd be well on my way to paying for the honeymoon of Jasmine's dreams." He turned to Jacob. "Have you and Mariana thought that far ahead?"

Taking discussion of weddings and honeymoons as his cue to leave, Daniel handed Jet his remaining chips. "Here, hope you have better luck than I did. Guess I'm not much of a gambler."

He was halfway across the room when his phone vibrated. Knowing he wouldn't be able to hear anyone in the makeshift casino, he increased his pace. When he saw Nicole's name on the screen, it was all he could do not to sprint for the door.

"Hello?" he pressed a hand to his other ear to block out as much noise as possible.

"D-Daniel?" The sound of her trembling voice sliced right through him.

"What is it? What's wrong?"

She sniffed. "Nothing major. I hope. I just needed… She didn't want me to worry Lizzie or the others, but I had to call someone. We're at the hospital. Me and Adele," she clarified. "She had this weird reaction at dinner that she's never had before, and I was afraid it might be anaphylactic and they tell you in all the information for postcancer follow-up care to see a doctor in case of wheezing or trouble breathing or—"

"Hey," he interrupted softly. "You sound like you're the one having trouble breathing. Slow down, honey." He sat on a padded bench in a quiet hotel corridor, wishing with his entire being that he could put his arms around her right now.

He heard her shaky intake of breath and slow, measured release.

"Sorry for flipping out on you," she said. "Adele and I went to dinner, and a few minutes after the main course was served, her face started swelling and she couldn't stop coughing. Being here at the hospital with her triggered so many bad memories…"

She stopped, took another deep breath. She was finally starting to sound like herself. "I wanted to call Lizzie and Chris, but Adele was adamant we not make this seem like a big deal if it's just some bizarre food allergy we didn't know about before. The E.R. doctor's no oncologist, but he said chemo alters a body and he's heard of instances where cancer survivors develop strange new allergies after treatment."

"I take it they got her reaction under control?" If not, he imagined Nicole would still be at her side, refusing to let anyone chase her out of Adele's room.

"Yeah. They gave her a shot for the hives and have her under observation. I should probably get back in there with her. I just needed a moment."

"Which hospital are you at? I'll meet you there."

"Don't you have Luke's bachelor party tonight?"

"I was on my way out, anyway."

She was quiet, and he heard the refusal in the pause before the words actually came. "Thanks, but it's pointless of you to drive over here if they're going to be releasing her soon. I shouldn't have called."

He scowled. "Of course you should have! You've already seen her through a traumatic health scare, and watching her get sick again—even if it's something minor—understandably stressed you out. I'm glad you called. Stress isn't good for you and the babies." Frankly, he thought it was selfish of Adele that she hadn't let Nicole call in his stepsiblings for moral support. The woman hadn't wanted to worry her own children, but she'd been okay with Nicole shouldering the anxiety by herself? "Are you *sure* you don't want me to come?"

"Positive. I'm better now. I drove us here calmly, I accessed all her patient information that I keep stored on my phone, filled out the forms. I was holding it together just fine, but then… Temporary anomaly. I really am okay."

That made one of them. Even after he disconnected the call, he felt shaky from the adrenaline that had surged through him when he'd heard her distress. She'd sounded so fragile. It had been the only time in his whole life he'd desperately wanted to be at a hospital. *But she doesn't want you there.* The irony churned like acid in his stomach.

As he'd watched his siblings over the past year, he'd told himself that, unlike Jet and Luke and Jacob, he wouldn't emotionally bind himself to a woman, so he could avoid moments like these. He'd allowed himself a strictly temporary fling with Nicole, secure in the knowledge that it would end soon and he wouldn't have to field emergency calls and pregnancy scares and parenting woes.

Yet now it occurred to him that there was something even worse than facing potential tragedy alongside someone you cared about—*not* being there and worrying that she faced it alone.

Chapter Ten

Daniel cut through the water with a blind ferocity that would no doubt vex his physical therapist, each stroke like a swing at an unseen enemy. Last night had been the worst sleep he'd had since his hospital stay after his injury in the rodeo ring.

Maybe he would have been better off remaining at the bachelor party because when he reached his house, the quiet solitude had rung in his ears more punishingly than the distorted casino music. He'd tried to call Nicole once, but she hadn't answered her phone. Maybe reception had been lousy in the hospital or she'd been busy trying to help Adele with something. When he finally gave up on the idea of her calling him back, he'd gone to bed, where he'd been plagued with nightmares.

Jumbled memories of his mom's death mixed with the image of Nicole sitting alone, crying in a hospital corridor. He'd been standing next to her, calling her name, but she hadn't been able to hear him. Around three in the morning, he'd awakened feeling dejected and heartsick. He'd turned on a late-night movie, but must have fallen asleep sometime before dawn. He woke hours later on the couch, troubled by a crick in his neck and creepy, lingering scenes of a terrified Nicole giving birth in an abandoned hospital.

He'd cooked himself brunch just to have something to do, then realized he had no appetite and headed for the ranch so he could exorcise his demons in the pool. He knew that Kim and Lizzie were hosting Carly's shower here this afternoon, but that was still a couple of hours away. So he was surprised to hear female voices above the splash of his body through the water.

Reaching the other end, he did a roll underwater and kicked off the concrete. Then he headed back to the shallow end and stood. If Lizzie had arrived to start setting up, maybe he could help her. That should keep him from compulsively dialing Nicole to see how she and Adele were doing.

Lizzie was nowhere to be seen, however. Jasmine stood on the porch next to Nicole, who looked absolutely beautiful in a deep green dress. Without pausing, he took the pool steps two at a time and went straight to her.

She let out a startled yelp when he hugged her. "Um...hi?"

Jasmine poked him in the side. "You do know you're all wet, right? It's one of the side effects of time in the pool."

He released Nicole, but couldn't tear his gaze off her. "I was worried about you."

Her eyes widened at the intensity of his tone. "I told you I was okay," she whispered. "I'm sorry I didn't call you back. By the time I got your voice mail, it was pretty late. I didn't want to bother you."

It was on the tip of his tongue to tell her she was allowed to bother him, that she should call anytime. But the words felt hypocritical and drastic. Once spoken, they couldn't be unsaid, and being someone's emergency phone call was the kind of responsibility he'd always shied away from. So he bit his tongue, wondering if being a coward was better than a hypocrite. Nicole deserved better than either.

"Daniel?" Her expression softened. Was she interpreting his silence as further evidence of deep concern?

Aware that Jasmine was openly staring at him and that he was behaving like a sleep-deprived lunatic, he struggled for a casual tone. "How come you're here so early? Did I get the time of the shower wrong?"

"No, Jasmine and I decided to meet here to talk twin stuff since we had trouble finding time during the week that worked for both of us. Jet's meeting his mother for coffee, so he'll bring Adele in time for the shower and I can drive her home later."

He'd forgotten that Jet hadn't gone with the girls to see Adele earlier in the week. For his stepbrother's sake, he hoped the reunion went well. Life took some bizarre twists—if Adele hadn't walked out on her children all those years ago, would he and Nicole ever have met?

"Well, I should probably get going then, let you and Jasmine chat."

"Don't let us run you off," Jasmine said. "We were going to sit at the table since it's pretty out, and Anna's bringing a pitcher of tea and some muffins. But you certainly won't be bothering anyone in the pool."

"It's okay. I was done with my workout anyway." That was true, more or less. He'd been desperate to relieve the tense, helpless frustration that had coiled inside him during the night. Seeing Nicole had done a lot to accomplish that.

Jasmine cleared her throat. "You know what? Anna's really busy working on the cake for the shower." When Daniel had come through the house earlier, Alex had been trying to convince the housekeeper to let him taste test all the goodies for the shower, and Julieta had told Brock he should take her son to the nature and science museum for the afternoon.

"I'll just get the muffins and tea myself," Jasmine continued. Then she disappeared into the house.

Nicole blinked. "Well. That was a painfully transparent attempt to give us time alone."

"I for one am grateful." He took her hands between both of his. "Now, tell me the truth. Are you really all right?"

She lowered her gaze, looking flustered by his concern. "Hey, Adele was the one who had the reaction," she joked. "I was just the driver. They think she's developed a sensitivity to eggs. There was some in her Caesar dressing. She'll be careful what she eats for the rest of our time here and follow up with an allergist when she's back in San Antonio."

He waited expectantly. Although he hoped Adele's allergic reaction was a fluke and not a sign of anything more ominous, his chief concern was Nicole, not her boss.

She sighed. "My calling you was a total overreaction and, having had time to sleep on it, I feel foolish. I had this weird moment of déjà vu and claustrophobia where it felt like the hospital walls were closing around me."

"Trust me, I know exactly what you mean. I can't stand hospitals. I mean, they're probably not anyone's favorite destination spot, but ever since my mom…" He tried to shove aside the painful memories, but it was difficult with last night's bad dreams so fresh in mind.

He changed the subject. "While we have a moment to ourselves, can I add that I've been thinking about you since we said goodbye at the mall?" The awkward way they'd left things after their shopping trip had rattled him. "I want to see you again."

When she didn't immediately answer, foreboding slithered through him. "Nicole? Has something changed? Did I—"

"You didn't do anything wrong," she said, anticipating his question. "And…I'd like to spend more time with you, too. I've missed you."

The last of his tension melted away. Unable to stop himself, not caring if Jasmine or Anna or anyone else saw, he cupped her face and kissed her. That kiss felt more like coming home than driving up to his dark house last night had. Her fingers clutching his bare shoulders reminded him sharply that he wore only a pair of bathing trunks. She felt so damn good against him, it took all his willpower not to suggest they go find a place where she could be equally shirtless.

He straightened, trying to look nonchalant and not like a man considering throwing her over his shoulder caveman style. They could be at his house in three minutes… "So you're still my date for Carly's wedding?"

"Absolutely." She gave him an impish smile. "I need

excuses to wear as many cute dresses as I can while I still fit into them."

He grinned. "In that case, I think I get to bring a plus-one to the rehearsal dinner, too. But that's not until next Saturday. Will I have to wait that long to see you?"

On Friday, he was leaving for Colorado and would return Saturday afternoon in plenty of time for the rehearsal and wedding on Sunday. Nicole and Adele planned to be back in San Antonio by the new year. His time with her was rapidly slipping away.

"I don't want to wait that long, either," she said. "But the next couple of days are pretty busy. Tomorrow, Adele and I are taking everyone from the Dallas staff to see the *Nutcracker* and then dinner in Reunion Tower. It's pretty much our version of an office Christmas party. And, of course, another excuse for a great dress. Monday's booked, too."

"You're telling me we have to wait until Tuesday?"

She gave him a rueful smile. "Yeah, I think so."

He kissed her forehead. "Luckily, you are worth the wait. Now, if you'll excuse me, I'm going to dive back into the pool." He suddenly had a different type of frustration in need of an outlet.

NICOLE HAD BROUGHT a small spiral notebook with her for her chat with Jasmine. As the time for the shower approached, she realized she'd filled lots of the pages with advice and product recommendations. One of Jasmine's key suggestions was to find a local club for moms of multiples and attend even when the thought of trying to get herself and two infants ready to leave the house seemed impossible. Jasmine assured her that the moral support and friendship she'd find there would be entirely worth it.

Admittedly, the thought of having a network of people she could talk to was heartening. Nicole was well liked and respected among her peers in San Antonio, but she was only just starting to realize how much she'd distanced herself from her social circle while taking care of Adele. Now she was feeling adrift. Twins were going to be a lot to handle by herself.

Jasmine had cautioned her to accept help whenever it was offered. "Don't be proud. And two newborns go through supplies like you will not believe! At the hospital, they'll give you some freebies like diapers and wipes or lotion samples. Take it all! Take anything you can legally get out the door with you. If it turns out to be something you don't use, you can always give it to one of your new buddies at the multiples club, but you cannot be too prepared. You must stock up on supplies—we're talking zombie-apocalypse-level stockpiling! Only, in this case, you're going to feel like the zombie. At least for the first few months. But I promise you, it gets easier."

On the table, Jasmine's phone pinged and she glanced down, then back up with an expression that was both hopeful and nervous. "Jet texted. He and Adele just pulled onto the Roughneck property. Do you want to go out front and meet them? I can't imagine being in her shoes and coming back here. I'm sure she'd appreciate the friendly face."

Nicole nodded. "Did he happen to mention how it went?"

Jasmine shook her head. "No idea. But no matter

how well it went, I doubt that many years apart can be bridged during one coffee meeting. I imagine the situation will take lots of patience."

Nicole smiled. "You are very wise."

"Well." The woman returned the smile, her eyes twinkling. "Jet's not marrying me for *just* my good looks."

They rounded the house in time to see Jet pulling up with Lizzie driving behind him. Jasmine went immediately to kiss her fiancé hello, and Nicole studied Adele's face, which looked splotchy. After careful scrutiny, Nicole decided her friend's features were tear-stained and that the blotches weren't an indication of another hives outbreak.

"Did it not go well?" she asked Adele softly.

Adele swallowed. "It was the most difficult thing I've ever done." That was saying something, given her medical history. "But, overall, it went better than I had any right to expect. Jet said that, if his father and Julieta agree, we should come for Christmas, that family should be together."

"Huh." In the abstract, Nicole didn't disagree. But wouldn't that be terribly awkward with Brock and his new wife in the same room? She assumed Carly had spoken to her father about Adele coming to the wedding, but she had no idea how that conversation had gone.

While Jet introduced his mother to Jasmine, Nicole went to greet Lizzie and a pretty young woman with warm brown eyes. Lizzie pronounced her "Kim Healy, cohost extraordinaire" and Carly's best friend since the two girls had tried to punch each other's lights out in second grade. Nicole laughed at that. When Daniel had told her during one of their dinners that the only one who'd rivaled him in the troublemaking department was Carly, she'd thought he'd been exaggerating. Maybe not.

Lizzie and Kim were pulling bags of decorations and door prizes out of the trunk.

"Anything I can do to help?" Nicole volunteered.

"You want to take these rolls of toilet paper?" Lizzie suggested. "They're lightweight." When Nicole stepped forward, Lizzie added under her breath, "Do we know how it went with Jet and Ad...with Mom?"

Hearing Lizzie call Adele that almost brought tears to Nicole's eyes. Her mother's struggle with addiction had been a harsh lesson that people were not always capable of changing who they were, even when they were motivated. But at least the Barons were proving that people were capable of compassion and forgiveness.

"I think it must have gone all right," Nicole speculated. "He mentioned her coming over on Christmas." It would be a nice chance for Adele to meet her grandchildren before Carly's wedding.

Lizzie looped her arm through Nicole's. "Then you'll join us, too, right? You can't spend Christmas alone in some efficiency apartment downtown."

Jasmine sent Nicole a teasing grin. "Her joining us can be Daniel's gift this year. He's out in the pool, and you should have seen the way he looked at her! His expression was scorching enough that Anna could have cooked with it!"

Nicole could feel the prickly heat of a blush spreading across her face, worsening when she realized Adele had overheard Jasmine, too. "It's not… We aren't…"

Laughing, Kim shook her head. "Another Baron falls, huh? Unbelievable. Is there something in y'all's water supply I don't know about?"

They headed toward the house, happily chatting, and Nicole didn't want to be churlish by correcting Kim. Daniel hadn't "fallen" for her. That wasn't the kind of relationship they had. At least, it wasn't supposed to be.

But even though she knew better than to let herself fall for him, was she growing dangerously dependent on him? During her brief panic attack at the hospital, Daniel had been the person she'd wanted to comfort her—the only person she'd wanted. *You're smarter than this, Nic.* If anyone should be good at insulating her emotions so that she didn't get hurt when it was time to say goodbye, it was the girl who'd lived in a parade of foster homes.

She'd understood the rules between her and Daniel since before he'd asked her to his house for dinner.

Have fun. Store up memories for long, lonely nights ahead. But do not get attached.

DRIED OFF AND once again wearing street clothes, Daniel was ready to leave the Roughneck. He thought about taking the long way around the outside of the house so that he didn't interrupt the women inside, but, technically, the party hadn't started yet. And he couldn't resist saying goodbye to Nicole.

When Julieta saw him in the kitchen, she narrowed her eyes in a mock-stern expression. "I'm guarding the food while Anna cleans up and changes clothes. We figured we were safe once I chased Brock and Alex out of the house, but if your hand reaches for anything on this kitchen island, prepare to get snapped with a dish towel."

He laughed. "I have no designs on the food, I swear. I was about to head home."

"All right then. See you Christmas Eve?"

"Yes, ma'am."

He followed the sounds of female laughter into the spacious front living room.

Carly waved a finger at him when she saw him. "Hey, this is a no-man zone." But she was smiling when she said it.

"I—"

From the foyer behind them, Brock's voice boomed. "Don't mind me. Got halfway there and realized I forgot my wall— What in the hell is *she* doing in my house?"

Daniel spun around in time to see his stepfather's face turn a mottled red with fury. He was glaring across the room at where Adele sat between Lizzie and Savannah.

Both sisters swung their gazes to Carly.

"I thought you talked to him!" Lizzie scolded.

"Julieta was going to help me find the right time," Carly said. Her hands went to her hips, and she straightened, her tone defensive. "Fine, I've been procrastinating for a few days. That's nothing compared to the *years* he had to tell us that our mother had come back to see us and that *he sent her away.* But you'll notice how that never came up!" It was still a source of contention that Carly had discovered from an old family friend how Brock had never told his children he'd forbidden Adele any contact with them.

Adele paled, looking stricken by the hostility in the room. "Maybe I should—"

Daniel stepped forward, taking advantage of his position between Brock and the spirited, hot-tempered daughter who was so much like him. "Carly, you have a bridal shower starting in ten minutes. I'll help your dad find his wallet."

"It's not lost," Brock said as Daniel gripped his arm and marched him past the room.

"Semantics. The fact remains, this is a no-man zone."

"It's my house!" Brock pulled away from him at the end of the hall. "And that woman isn't welcome under my roof. You weren't here when she left. You don't have the first damn clue what those kids—"

"Don't I?" Daniel snapped in a low tone. "Are you forgetting that my mom died? I know *exactly* what it's like to have your mother ripped away from you, one day there, the next day gone."

The older man looked shamefaced but didn't back down. "That was different. Peggy, God rest her soul, died. She never would have abandoned you willingly. Delia made a conscious choice to walk away from little ones who needed her. Who cried for her for months."

Brock shoved a hand through his hair. "I sure as hell couldn't fill the hole for them. Not any more than I could for you and Jacob after your mama's death. I excel at a great many things—rodeo, making money. But parenting…" He didn't meet Daniel's gaze as he stumbled through the halting words. "It's been pointed out to me repeatedly in the past year that I've…made mistakes."

Daniel blinked, stunned. Brock Baron was not a man who easily admitted he was wrong. Maybe he could be reasoned with, after all.

"Don't let today turn into a mistake," Daniel urged his stepfather. "I know how much you love Carly. Don't you want her to be happy?"

"Of course! I—"

"Well, it's important to her that her mother be part of the wedding celebration. You kept them apart once. If you've ever regretted that decision, now's your chance to atone. Don't try to keep them apart now. Carly and the others…they're adults. They have to make their own choices about the relationship they want with Adele."

"Maybe. But when you have children of your own, you'll understand," Brock said gruffly. "Adult or not, they are still my kids."

They. Not *you.* But that didn't matter right now. This wasn't about Daniel not feeling like a true part of the family, it was about repairing a rift between people he cared for. Maybe Nicole's compassion was rubbing off on him.

"Well." Julieta stomped toward them, holding Brock's wallet out. "That was quite a spectacle you caused. Are you going to leave peacefully, or do I need to escort you to your truck?"

Daniel smothered a laugh. Julieta might be the only person on the planet who could make Brock look nervous. Thank God she had a big heart. He knew she would campaign for the Baron siblings to reunite with their mother.

"I'm going," Brock said. He jerked his head in Daniel's direction. "This one already talked some sense into me."

Julieta raised an eyebrow. "Did you, now? Then I take back what I said earlier about the dish towel. You've earned the right to sample some of the goodies in the kitchen."

"I'm honored, but I'm just going to head out." Food didn't sound that appealing. Although everything seemed to have been handled for now, residual tension knotted his stomach. Even when he'd seen Brock in the hospital, the man hadn't seemed as vulnerable as he had when he'd admitted that he hadn't known how to be there for his kids.

For years, Daniel had resented feeling like a second-class citizen and questioned whether his stepfather cared about him. But the situation had been complicated. Maybe Brock had cared and simply hadn't been good at expressing himself, how to reach out to two motherless boys and ease the loss they'd felt. Their brief, heated conversation in the hall had been unexpectedly candid. It was also the closest Daniel had ever felt to the man. A shame that, if Daniel moved to Colorado, there wouldn't be many opportunities to develop that bond further.

Chapter Eleven

As Daniel stood outside the front door of the Rough-neck, eyeing the wreath that was almost as tall as his nephew, it occurred to him that one of the advantages of rodeo life had been frequent travel, which afforded easy excuses. Everyone had understood if he missed a birthday party or Brock and Julieta's anniversary when he was on the road. But it was much harder to manu-facture a reason not to come to the house for Christmas Eve dinner now that the biggest demands on his time were physical rehab and sending out résumés. He hadn't been to the ranch since that unexpectedly emo-tional confrontation with Brock and he felt almost… nervous about the family gathering tonight.

The door swung open, and Anna greeted him with a pink-cheeked smile. He wondered affectionately if she'd already had a glass of the infamous eggnog, which Jet had dubbed the "pa-Rum-pa-Rum-Rum." "Come on in! Everyone else is here already. Well, ex-cept your brother, of course."

Jacob and Mariana weren't due back from Austin until tomorrow. The house was full of noise—happy squeals of children hoping Santa would visit tonight, the whirr of some kitchen appliance, Travis and Luke laughing at something Jet had said in the adjoining room. With all the extra people under the roof this year, it was the biggest Christmas Eve in Baron history. And, for a staggering second, Daniel felt completely isolated. Without his big brother to help bridge the gap, he felt even more disconnected from his stepsiblings than usual.

When Peggy had still been alive, she'd established the tradition of serving Christmas Eve dinner in the late afternoon rather than at night. That way, there was plenty of time to attend the local church's nativity play and still get the kids in bed early so Santa could visit. Daniel could scarcely imagine the amount of pre-Christmas-morning assembly required on gifts for six children. With Alex only five, and his cousins even younger than that, the tradition of an early supper and early bedtimes still worked well today. By the time they finished eating, it probably wouldn't even be dark outside.

Maybe part of the reason Daniel felt so restless was that he was antsy for night to fall. Nicole, who'd spent the night last night, was coming over later so they could have their own Christmas Eve celebration. He knew she was coming out to the ranch tomorrow with Adele, but Christmas at the Roughneck would be a madhouse. It would be next to impossible to steal much private time with her, and they had only a few days left.

"Hey." Carly approached, surprising him with a hug. "Thanks for the other day. That could have gotten really ugly if you hadn't been there."

"You're welcome. You're giving me too much credit though. Lizzie or Julieta would have stepped in."

"Probably," she agreed. "But whatever you said to Daddy... Well, he won't be founding an Adele Black Fan Club anytime soon, but he's making an effort. He even said that, if I wanted, she could sit in the front pew at the wedding with him and Julieta. I owe you."

He was still bemused by her praise when Lizzie came up a few minutes later, echoing her sister's words.

And a few minutes after that, Jet nudged him in the side. "You saved my neck, bro. I never would have invited Adele to come over for Christmas if I'd realized Carly still hadn't squared away her presence with Dad. That could have been painfully awkward."

Daniel couldn't help a wry laugh. "You weren't there for the shower encounter. It *was* painfully awkward. And loud."

"Well, that's our family. We Barons don't do anything halfway, right? Come on, let's get you a drink."

As it got closer to time to eat, Julieta began assigning orders. She instructed Travis and Luke to move some extra chairs to the table and asked Alex to get the butter dish out of the refrigerator. Savannah was in charge of stirring gravy on the stove, so forth and so on. Daniel felt a little useless waiting for an assignment. He thought about just taking the initiative to jump in and help, but experience with that many Barons in the kitchen had taught him that sometimes what one person thought of assistance was another person's definition of getting in the way.

"If you need me to do anything," he called to Julieta,

"my shoulder's a lot better. Sierra says she's impressed with my progress."

Brock stepped up to him, swirling a scotch and soda around in his highball glass. "Glad to hear it. And what does your physical therapist say about when you can start riding again?" He glanced away, then met Daniel's gaze. "Maybe I don't say it enough, but you do a damn fine job in the rodeo ring. Always been proud of your standings."

Daniel winced inwardly. Now that he'd decided to give up rodeo, he wouldn't be able to use that particular subject to connect with his stepfather.

"But you want to pick it up again nice and easy," Brock advised. "Log plenty of time in the practice ring before you get too ambitious."

"Actually…" He swallowed. "I'm not planning to go back to rodeo."

Would Brock be confused? Annoyed? Rodeo was in the Baron blood. *Which doesn't actually flow through your veins.*

Instead, the man took a deep breath, then nodded, his expression pensive. "Is that why I got a call from Chuck Bowlan? Seems someone asked him about a reference for you." Brock was a powerful man who had a vast network of business contacts and former rodeo buddies that spanned the state.

Daniel nodded. "I'm looking for something more concrete than sporadic horse training." He could continue investing in rodeo stock and splitting the profits with his friends, but that wasn't enough to keep him busy. "I was planning to tell everyone after Christmas and Carly's wedding that I'm looking. But nothing's happened yet. I haven't interviewed or received any offers."

"Well—" Brock peered over the rim of his glass, carefully evaluating Daniel "—when you do start interviewing, offers will follow. Any ranch would be lucky to have you. You have a rare understanding of horses and a strong work ethic. Now that you've matured and aren't such a damn hothead, you're a real asset."

"Thanks." Daniel grinned. As far as Christmas Eve compliments went, it wasn't terribly sentimental, but Brock's statement had been accurate. Daniel *was* more levelheaded now. He tried to be pragmatic and detached, not letting emotion goad him into mistakes the way it had during his adolescence. He was very controlled.

And that's why you've been fidgeting like a three-year-old hopped up on sugar cookies and espresso, counting the seconds until you can get out of here and be with Nicole? Maybe his pragmatic discipline didn't extend to her.

He'd actually had an insane moment yesterday where he'd thought about asking if she'd ever seen Colorado and inviting her to go with him on his interview trip, even though she had details she was still wrapping up on her wind farm project and this visit would involve two flights in two days. It had dawned on him that appropriate stocking stuffers for a woman one was casually seeing included scented lotions or gift cards to bookstores—not plane tickets. The problem was, where Nicole was concerned, his feelings grew less casual with every passing day.

"I CAN'T BELIEVE you got a tree!"

Daniel bobbed his head in modest acknowledgment as if it was no big deal, but he'd known she would love it.

"I was here just yesterday," Nicole pointed out. "I can't believe you were able to find one on Christmas Eve."

For her, he would have chopped one down if necessary. "Actually, it turns out that if you wait until the day before Christmas, you can get a pretty sweet sales price on the remaining inventory. But since I got a tree in your honor, it's only fair that you help me decorate it. I retrieved those when I was at the ranch this afternoon." He indicated the boxes sitting against the far wall of his living room.

The boxes contained some of his mother's things, including her favorite Christmas keepsakes and ornaments that he and Jacob had made for her when they were kids. Maybe sometime after Christmas, he and Jacob could go through the boxes together and divide the contents equally. For now, Daniel had simply wanted to hang some decorations for his celebration with Nicole.

She walked over to the boxes and knelt down to remove a lid. Amid the more elegant jewel-toned glass balls were a Styrofoam horseshoe decorated in uneven clumps of glitter and a frame made of spray-painted macaroni that held a picture of him as a buck-toothed seven-year-old.

Her breath caught. "These were your mom's?"

"Well, someone should be using them, right?" He swallowed, remembering his mom's smile, the vanilla-scented perfume she'd favored and the way she'd insisted on a round of Christmas hugs before anyone was allowed to open a gift. "She loved them, and they've just been sitting neglected in an attic for years. You know I'm not really one for decorating my place at Christmas, but...I wanted to share these with you."

She came to him, threading her fingers through his hair and kissing him softly. His body responded with instant need. They'd made love last night and again this morning before she left. He shouldn't be this hungry for her, but the more they were together, the more he wanted. She gently scraped her teeth across the side of his neck, then kissed her way down to the collar of his shirt.

He groaned. "Okay, forget the tree, then." Clasping her hand, he took a step toward his bedroom.

"Wait, no." She stood her ground, although the expression in her gaze told him she wanted him every bit as much as he craved her. "You went to the trouble to do this nice surprise for me, and I'm ruining it."

Her skewed summary startled a bark of laughter from him. "Yeah. I hate when a beautiful woman wants to make love to me. Nothing ruins Christmas faster than that."

She grinned. "Then prepare to have your Christmas thoroughly and enthusiastically ruined. But, *after* we finish this."

He let her return to the boxes, enjoying her good mood. She pulled out a clump of white and red construction paper pieces that had been glued together in a shape generously described as a candy cane. Daniel's name was scrawled on one side of the ornament in crayon.

"Wow." Her eyes sparkled. "If you hadn't become a badass cowboy, you might have had a real career in art."

He started to tease her back, to make a retort about how no one's second-grade artwork was perfect and how he was sure she had some peppermint skeletons in her closet, too. But then it occurred to him that she probably didn't. Who had held on to Nicole's keepsakes over the years? Report cards, watercolor paintings, small family knickknacks that were meant to be hers someday?

Recalling how out of place and anxious to leave he'd felt at the Christmas Eve dinner made him a little ashamed. What would Nicole have given for a holiday like that? He vowed that tomorrow, no matter how much of a madhouse it was and what familial drama might occur when Brock and Adele were in the same room, he would make the day special for Nicole.

When she caught him staring at her, he said, "My mom would have really liked you."

"Thank you." As her smile faded, she bit her lip. "I'm not sure my mother has the capacity to like anyone. How can you if you don't have the foundation of liking yourself first? It's taken me a lot of years not to take it personally that her self-loathing was stronger than her love for me." She shook her head. "But I'm not wasting any of our Christmas Eve together being sad! Can I give you your presents now?" She bounced on the balls of her feet, looking as excited as Rosie or Alex or Cody about the idea of gifts.

"Presents, plural? Careful, you're gonna spoil me."

"Be right back." Then she was out the front door, and he watched her pull a large red gift bag out of the car. When she came back inside, he saw that she also had a much smaller package tucked under her arm. He opened the kitchen drawer where he'd hidden a tiny box earlier in the day.

They sat on the couch together. Nicole tucked her feet under her, beaming at him. "Open the big one first," she instructed.

"Okay." He tore aside the tape and curling ribbon. As he dug through a thin layer of gold tissue paper, it became clear he was unwrapping a blanket of some kind. There was dark fringe around the edges and some kind of picture emblazoned across it, but he had to stand up and shake out the tapestry-style blanket to get a clear look.

A yellow-eyed owl stood on a tree branch glaring back at him.

Nicole gave him a solemn look, placing a hand over her heart. "Isn't it time to start the healing?" she deadpanned.

He arched an eyebrow, trying not to laugh. "You're a very mean person."

"You have to bring the blanket to the ranch tomorrow. Jacob will want to see it," she predicted.

"You're both very mean people."

She handed him the smaller box. "Here, maybe this will help make up for my cruel streak."

Inside he found a CD. The plastic case had several signatures scrawled across it in silver marker. It was an album from that indie band out of Austin that they both liked.

"I pulled some strings and got you an autographed copy of their next album. It doesn't go on sale for another week and a half."

"This is perfect." He knew instinctively that he'd think of her whenever he was listening to the songs. The memories would be bittersweet. "Thank you. Now your turn."

She looked surprised by the obvious jewelry box but made a joke, keeping her tone light. "Is it a pony?" All the teasing went out of her expression when she lifted the sterling silver necklace out of the box. Hanging from the chain was a heart pendant; linked inside the larger heart were two smaller, rose-gold hearts.

"To symbolize you and the babies," he said awkwardly. When he'd seen it in a display window, he'd known immediately that she had to have it.

"Daniel, it's beautiful." She stood. "Help me put it on?"

He got to his feet and swept her hair aside, trying to work the delicate clasp. It was difficult, distracted as he was by her nearness. Once he got the necklace fastened, he didn't let her go. Instead, he dotted kisses down the base of her neck, listening to the change in her breathing, completely attuned to the chemistry between them. She turned her head, craning upward to kiss him.

With one hand anchored around her midsection, he pressed her close to him. When his other hand slipped beneath the hem of her sweater, trailing across her silky skin until he'd reached the curve of her breast, she demonstrated her approval with a slow, provocative twist of her hips, rubbing against his erection. He shuddered, closing his eyes to focus all his senses on the feel of her. She repeated the motion, this time even slower, a purposeful, sensual tease. He tightened his hold on her breast, squeezing the tight nipple between his finger and thumb.

She murmured his name in a low, throaty purr.

With his mouth at her ear, he whispered, "Can we please go ruin Christmas now?"

"Lead the way, cowboy."

Chapter Twelve

Nicole's initial trepidation about feeling like an interloper, and her unspoken worry about residual hostile feelings between Adele and Brock, didn't last any longer than the time it took to get past the foyer. Julieta Baron came forward to hug her soundly.

"Nicole!" Her richly accented voice was warm and welcoming. "It is always so good to see to you." Then Julieta turned to greet the original mistress of this house. She took Adele's hand in both of hers and smiled with no trace of hostility or judgment. "And Adele. We are glad you could join us today."

Behind his wife, Brock Baron looked slightly less glad, but he gave a terse nod of welcome just the same. "Delia."

"Adele," she corrected without rancor. "I've worked hard to put the woman I was—and her mistakes—behind me."

After a brief hesitation, he nodded. "We all make mistakes. I've made some I wish I could take back, too." With that, he turned to one of the grandchildren who was barreling through the room and asked the child to demonstrate her new toy.

Adele, who'd spent the drive here worried about a repeat of the shower confrontation, expelled a relieved breath and looked at Julieta. "Thank you for agreeing to have me here. And for taking care of him. I can tell you're a good influence."

Julieta led them into a living room where chaos reigned. Lights and sounds from half a dozen different toys competed with laughter and stories being told about Christmases past; underscoring all of it, jazzy Christmas carols played through the speakers mounted in each corner.

"Mom!" Carly spotted Adele first and came forward to hug her. "Merry Christmas."

"Thank you, darling. Merry Christmas to you, too. I have presents for everyone in the car, but I wasn't sure if I should bring them in yet." Her exact words to Nicole had been that the sight of gift bags to preschoolers was like blood in the water for sharks. Adele hadn't wanted to cause a frenzy.

"We'll send Jet and Luke out for them in a bit," Carly said. "Come meet everyone." Her smile widened. "I can't wait to introduce you to Rosie."

Across the room, Daniel sat on the arm of a crowded sofa. As soon as he saw Nicole, he got up and came toward her. The way his eyes locked with hers made her feel like the most important person in the room.

He kissed her, then caught one of the curls that spilled over her shoulder, tugging gently. "Finally. Now that you're here, my Christmas is perfect."

"Finally? You saw me just a few hours ago," she reminded him. His method of waking her up was the best present any girl could ask for.

"I'd like to see that much of you again." He grinned, waggling his eyebrows in comic innuendo. "Very soon. But for today, I'll be generous and share your company with other people."

They returned to the couch, where Jacob stood up to hug her and Jasmine offered to let Nicole have her seat. "The twins will love it if I'm sitting on the floor anyway," she said. "They think anyone over ten years old is a jungle gym."

Chris wished her a merry Christmas and told her that Lizzie was upstairs trying to get a fussy baby to fall asleep. "Apparently, this much activity is overstimulation for a baby. Go figure," he drawled, gesturing at the festive pandemonium around them.

Once she was seated, she asked Jacob, "Did your brother show you what I got him for Christmas?"

Jacob laughed, and Daniel held out his hand. When Jacob pulled out his wallet, Daniel explained, "I knew you'd have to boast about that. Bet him ten bucks that you'd bring it up in the first five minutes you were here."

Daniel affected a troubled expression. "How am I supposed to sleep with one of those winged beasts in the house?"

She laughed, lowering her voice so the others didn't overhear. "I'm just sorry I won't be there to protect you."

"Me, too."

Spending the past two nights with him had been amazing, and not just because of the sex. They'd talked until the wee hours as they drifted to sleep, and he was so solicitous of her in the mornings, although her nausea seemed to be receding, thank God. Sleeping tonight in her room at the apartment was going to feel lonely. But his flight tomorrow was so early that it made no sense for her to go to his place tonight.

Probably just as well. It would be too easy to fall into the habit of waking up next to him. She needed to remind herself that they were going their separate ways soon. This week, it might feel perfectly natural to start the day in his arms. But this time next week? Daniel Baron would be nothing more than a wonderful memory.

"I DON'T THINK it's fair that you guys won," Daniel complained to Chris and Lizzie. "Nicole was the best artist on your team, but she's my guest. That's like using my secret weapon against me!" She'd even maintained her composure when her word to draw was *Bed* and Daniel hadn't been able to take his eyes off her. *Boots* had been another one that made her blush and made him want to drag her upstairs to an empty room.

Lizzie was cheerfully unsympathetic about the last-minute defeat of the other team. "Tough Tater Tots, Danny." She packed the board game into its box while Nicole and Chris high-fived their win. At another folding card table that had been moved into the living room, Brock and Julieta were playing Candy Land with some of the kids. Carly and Luke had announced they were going for a "walk" to the barn—then skedaddled before anyone could offer to join them—while Savannah and her mother worked a jigsaw puzzle at the dining room table. Barons were scattered throughout the house, a few of them napping.

And, surprisingly, it was the best day Daniel could remember in a very long time.

Nicole was ribbing Lizzie over the Tater Tots comment. "Is that what you say to whiny underlings at work, too? It sounds *very* executive."

"You laugh now," Mariana said, "but you have to get in the habit of modifying your language. Otherwise, when a kid gets to be Cody's age, they've already learned really interesting phrases to use in public places like the grocery store. Or church."

That explained why, when Jacob had banged his shin on the coffee table earlier, he'd let loose a nonsensical stream of words that included "holy shipyard."

Currently, Jacob was mock-glaring at his brother. "Don't be a sore loser. Especially since it's your fault we lost."

"How is it my fault?"

"We were one point away! That last picture I drew was clearly a toucan." He held up the pad of paper. "Check out the beak."

Daniel smirked. "I see. There were two teammates guessing, but only I'm getting blamed. If your drawing was so wonderful, how come Mariana didn't recognize what it was?"

Jacob slung an arm around his fiancée's shoulders. "Because she's blinded by love for me. And who can fault her for that?"

"And also," Mariana added in a stage whisper, "because his so-called toucan looked like a scythe."

Daniel chuckled, trying to remember the last time he'd had this much fun among his siblings and their significant others.

"I put it in the tree so you'd know it was a bird," Jacob said.

"Sorry." She gave him an apologetic smile. "It looked more like you were trying to chop a tree down."

"Maybe next time we should let Cody play with us," Daniel suggested. "He might do a better job."

Nicole shook her head woefully. "Wow, look how they turn on each other. It's painful to watch. I'm so glad I was on the other team. You know, the *winning* one."

Daniel started to playfully threaten that she should sleep with one eye open but then suddenly remembered she wouldn't be sleeping next to him tonight. The thought bothered him more than it should. He liked having her there. *What about her job?* She had to go back to San Antonio sooner or later. She couldn't stay simply because he liked ending his day with her. But the bigger problem wasn't geography. He was planning to leave Dallas, anyway. The bigger problem was that, in six months, it wouldn't just be Nicole falling asleep and waking up each day. It would be Nicole and two babies.

Almost as if underscoring his thoughts, the sound of Natalie crying came through the baby monitor. Lizzie poked her husband in the arm.

"Your turn for diaper duty," she reminded him.

"Actually," Nicole interrupted shyly, "would you mind if I gave it a try? I could use the practice."

Chris pumped his fist in the air. "Score!"

"You should still go with her and show her where everything is," Lizzie said.

Mariana and Jacob had wandered over to the other

table to cheer on Cody at his game, so Daniel and Lizzie were left alone. She watched Chris and Nicole leave the room, then turned back to Daniel.

"I knew Christopher thought highly of her when they worked together, and the more I get to know her, the more I see why. She's special."

"That she is." No question about it.

"And she's good for you. You're—don't take this the wrong way—friendlier when she's around. Not that you were unfriendly before, exactly, but you certainly smile a lot more now."

True. And he didn't think it was just because Nicole rounded him out, making him half of a couple so that he finally fit in with his married and engaged siblings. When she was happy, he found himself relaxed and at peace with the world around him. When she was stressed, as she had been the day she'd talked to the Barons about Adele's return, Daniel was too worried about her to focus on himself and whether he fit in.

"She told me the two of you are only casually dating," Lizzie said, her tone disappointed. "That's a lovely necklace you got her. Can't say *I* ever got jewelry from someone I casually dated for a couple of weeks."

"Well, she likes it, and that's the important part." He stood. "If you'll excuse me, I think I'm going to see if there are any of Anna's sugar cookies left in the kitchen."

Lizzie let him go without further comment, but he couldn't stop thinking about that necklace, about the hearts he'd given Nicole for Christmas. How much different would the situation be if he'd found the courage to give her his heart?

DECEMBER IN COLORADO was a hell of a lot colder than December in Texas. Daniel found himself grateful to his friend Bodie not only for picking him up at the airport and buying him lunch, but for loaning him a jacket more appropriate to the weather than the one Daniel had brought with him. Between Bodie's coat and Daniel's own gloves and boots, he managed to keep his teeth from chattering while talking to his potential future employer, Garrett Frost. To get a sense of Daniel's skills and rapport with animals, Garrett had taken him out on the Double F to tackle chores.

"I appreciate your agreeing to meet with me the day after Christmas," Daniel told the other man. "I hope I'm not intruding on your holiday."

"You know how it is on a ranch. There aren't many true days off. The banks and post offices may close, but animals still need to be fed, precautions against bad weather still need to be taken. Which is why we really need to find someone. Mom's convinced Dad to more or less retire. The physical work is starting to take a toll on him, especially in the winter. If Bodie and I try to make up the slack, we end up busy from sunup to sundown. And I need more time at home right now. My wife, Arden, recently had a baby. Our oldest daughter just turned one a couple of months ago, so you can imagine how busy they keep us. Sometimes, when I'm knee-deep in diapers, I wonder if this is what it feels like to have twins."

Daniel's mind drifted from the workings of the Double F Ranch back to Nicole. He'd sent her a text when he landed in Colorado, but he hadn't talked to her all day. If ever there was a woman capable enough to successfully handle twins, it was her. But he hated that she had to do so alone. For too much of her life—waiting for her mother to come back for her, not fully bonding with her foster families—she'd been alone. She deserved a partner, someone who loved and cherished her.

"Daniel?" Garrett paused, eyeing him curiously. "Did I lose you?"

"No. Sorry. I was just thinking of a friend of mine who's pregnant with twins."

"Well, good luck to her. I adore my daughters, but, man, they are a handful."

They'd reached the stables, so Daniel made an effort to put aside thoughts of Nicole and demonstrate his familiarity with horses. He talked about his training of Sugarhoof and several others in the past year, then switched to discussing his work with cattle.

"I'm definitely at my most comfortable working with livestock," he said. "I just don't want to ride them in the rodeo ring anymore."

After the tour and errands were completed, Garrett invited him into the main house for some hot coffee. A lovely brunette sat on a couch, cradling a sleeping infant. The woman waggled her fingers hello at Daniel.

"I'd get up to shake your hand," she said softly, "but she just fell asleep." To Garrett, she said, "Hope's in the kitchen with your mom, who, unless I'm mistaken, is letting her dig into the leftover icing from those gingerbread houses we made."

Garrett rolled his eyes. "Now that Dad's retired, I've got to talk them into travel. If they're here all the time, they are going to spoil the girls rotten."

Arden grinned, looking relatively untroubled by that

possibility. "They're the only grandparents. They're trying to squeeze in enough love for two sets." As if remembering they had company, Arden looked back at Daniel. "My parents died when I was young."

"Sorry to hear that." Missing his own mother had taught him that time eased the wound, but the ache never fully disappeared. No matter the months or years that passed, there would forever be bittersweet moments when you wished a loved one was there to share good news or milestones. But obviously the pain of losing her parents hadn't stopped Arden Frost from falling in love or building a happy life.

The two men stopped in the kitchen to collect cups of coffee, Garrett sparing a hug for his daughter, then went into the study, where the senior Mr. Frost joined them to discuss the recent expansion of the Double F and future plans. When they finished talking, Daniel was surprised to see that it was already growing dark outside. The Frosts invited him to stay for dinner, and by the time they finished, Daniel was reasonably certain they were going to offer him the job.

He spent the night on Bodie's couch, then met Garrett Frost for breakfast in town before his return flight.

Garrett smiled from the other side of the booth. "You passed the wife-and-mother test. They both liked you. And my father likes anyone who's good with the animals. He said he defers to my judgment there. If you want the job, it's yours."

Daniel was glad to have accomplished something outside the Baron sphere of influence, where his adopted name opened doors. He thought the ranch was well run and that the Frosts were nice people. This was exactly the kind of opportunity he'd hoped for when he made the decision not to return to rodeo. So…why was he hesitating?

"Can I have some time to think about it?" Daniel asked. "I'll call you with an answer no later than Monday."

"Fair enough," Garrett agreed.

Two hours later, as Daniel's plane powered down the runway and ascended into the air, he took a long look at the view below. Colorado was beautiful. But, deep down, he knew he wouldn't be returning anytime soon.

Traffic made it difficult to get from the airport to the wedding rehearsal in time, but since Daniel was only an usher, he figured they could get started without him. Hopefully, he was capable of escorting honored guests to their seats without too much practice. He slipped in the back of the church in time to watch Alex and Rosie practice walking down the aisle. They were truly adorable, and he experienced an unfamiliar pang at the sight of the solemn five-year-old and rambunctious toddler, who seemed to think it would be more fun to pirouette in forward-moving circles than walk a straight line.

Carly and her soon-to-be stepdaughter were well matched. He could *almost* imagine his stepsister deciding to spin in exuberant circles instead of taking the more orthodox route. However the bride got to the front of the sanctuary, Daniel imagined that Luke's expression of love would be the same. The Roughneck's ranch manager had loved Carly for a long time, and despite Daniel's usual cynicism, he was glad life had given them a second chance at their relationship.

Although, their relationship wasn't simply a quirk of

fate. That sounded passive. They'd had to actively work through their past history and overcome emotional obstacles to get where they were today—grinning in front of the altar, knowing that by this time tomorrow they'd be man and wife.

"Hey." At the back of the church, Lizzie poked him in the shoulder. "Are you all right? For a second there, I could have sworn you were getting misty-eyed."

"Please." He made a dismissive sound. "Manly cowboys don't get misty."

She laughed, pointing. "Tell that to Daddy." Brock Baron stood off to the side of the pews, sniffling loudly. This was his last daughter to settle down, his youngest. Wild child Carly would soon become the respectable Mrs. Luke Nobel.

Carly's other parent was not present for the rehearsal, but tomorrow, Daniel himself would escort Adele to a seat of honor, marked by one of the dark green pew bows. He knew it meant the world to Carly to have all of her parents present.

Finally, the rehearsal ended. People headed for their assorted vehicles, all eager for the dinner being held in the private room of an upscale steak house. Daniel found himself lengthening his stride, eager to cross the parking lot and reach his truck. Nicole was meeting him at the steak house, and he couldn't wait to see her.

While Mariana buckled Cody into the truck a few spaces away, Jacob came over to his brother. "How'd the interview go?" he asked quietly.

"Really well," Daniel said. "It's a great operation, and they offered me the position." He waited only a beat before admitting, "But I'm not going to take it. I think…I think I'm going to look for something a little closer to home."

Jacob clapped him on the back. "Glad to hear it. You know I would've supported your decision either way, but we'd miss you." His expression turned sly. "When you say 'closer to home,' do you by any chance mean closer to San Antonio?"

Daniel elected not to answer. But he was grinning as he steered his truck out of the lot, counting the minutes until he could kiss Nicole hello.

LEANING ON THE marble counter in the ladies' room, Nicole shot her reflection a reproving glare. *Get it together.* It hadn't mattered if she got weepy during the slide show that featured pictures of Carly and Luke growing up, because the lights had been dimmed. But now that the show was over and the waiters were about to serve the dessert course, people might notice that she was falling apart.

She'd been on an emotional roller coaster all day after not having slept well for the past two nights. It wasn't so much that Daniel hadn't been lying in the bed next to her that made her want to curl up in a ball—even in her heightened emotional state, she wasn't so far gone that she couldn't last two nights without him—but the knowledge that after tomorrow's wedding, their time together was over. They'd reached the end of the road.

Since they'd been surrounded by his family all night, she hadn't asked him about his interview. But even if discretion hadn't kept her silent, dread might have. Even as she acknowledged that they had no future, she hated imagining him so far away. If his enthusiastic kiss hello and nonstop smiling tonight were any indication, his interview had gone *really* well.

Then you should be happy for him. Just as she was happy that Adele had reunited with her children and would probably be spending a lot more time in Dallas from now on. And happy for herself, learning that she was going to be the mother of two babies! Yep, everything was coming together wonderfully.

So why am I crying in a steak house bathroom?

Taking a deep breath, she reached for the door, resolved to go back out there and be a fun date for the rest of the night. Since she was in town for only a few more days, she should make the most of them, not sabotage what precious time she and Daniel had left.

She was halfway across the restaurant when he walked up to her. Obviously, she'd been missing so long that he'd come looking for her. "Sorry," she said. "Seeing those baby pictures got me all choked up. I needed a minute."

"That's okay. Actually, I was hoping to steal a moment alone with you. I've got something I've been wanting to tell you all night."

"They offered you the job," she said numbly.

"Well, yes, but— Here, come with me." He led her to an unoccupied corner of the restaurant bar, settling her on a stool and leaning close. "They did offer me the job, but I'm going to turn it down. Colorado is too far away from you," he added, tipping her chin up with his thumb. "I don't want us just to be some holiday fling. You made this the best Christmas of my life. I don't want to give you up yet."

The word *yet* flashed like a glowing red warning sign. "So what's the plan, to hook up on the weekends and dump me when the babies are born?" The question spilled out uncensored, exposing her raw, ugly fears.

"No!" He straightened, looking startled. "Nicole, I thought you'd be happy about this. Did you miss me at all when I was gone?"

Yes. "It was only two days."

"Well, it was long enough for me to realize I'm falling in love with you."

Her heart stopped. They were the words she hadn't been able to admit she wanted to hear. The words that were too good to be true. But they were, after all, only words. None of the facts had changed. A couple of weeks ago he'd claimed he never wanted to marry or have kids, and now he was pledging his love for a woman pregnant with twins?

She cupped his face with her palm, unable to resist touching him. "Oh, Daniel. I want to believe that, but… This is a sentimental time for you right now. The big family holiday, Carly's wedding. You're surrounded by happy couples every time you turn around. It's easy to get caught up in that."

"That's not what this is."

"I grew up watching an addict. We had moments like these. She said a lot of things she probably meant at the time. But change isn't easy. It doesn't happen just because we had a lovely Christmas together. I spent my childhood waiting for her to clean up her act, to keep her promises, to come back for me. I can't do that again. What happens a few months down the road, when I've let myself rely on you and you realize that a relationship with the mother of two isn't what you want?"

"You can't know that will happen!"

"Just like you can't guarantee it won't. This—" she waved her hand between them "—has been fun. But it was a temporary escape from reality, nothing more. I have to start planning for three. You're a hell of a guy, Daniel Baron, but you were never part of those plans."

Chapter Thirteen

Half a whiskey over ice later, Daniel was still seated at the bar, trying to figure out what in the hell had happened. He'd told a woman he loved her—a woman he'd been nearly certain returned his feelings—and she'd ended their relationship. She'd compared him to the addict who'd abandoned her. How was that fair?

"Daniel?"

He swiveled at the sound of his brother's voice. "Hey."

"We've been trying to figure out where you and Nicole disappeared to."

"Nicole left." Her parting words had been that, under the circumstances, she didn't think she should be at the wedding. He wasn't going to see her tomorrow. If she had her way, he wouldn't ever see her again. It felt as if he'd fallen off his stool, through the floor and just kept plummeting. "Nicole left for good."

Jacob did a double take. "You mean she dumped you?"

"Not sure." He downed the last of the whiskey. "Do you have to be in a relationship to get dumped? Because we weren't. She made that very clear. We were 'fun.' And 'temporary.'" She'd reduced him to using air quotes. He'd hit rock bottom.

"Oh, boy." Jacob shifted his weight, looking uncomfortable, obviously wishing he had a way to help. "How about I let Mariana drive Cody home, and I ride with you? I could crash at your place tonight if you need someone to listen."

"Can we stop on the way and pick up more whiskey?"

Jacob winced. "Ordinarily, I'd say you were entitled, but you can't show up hungover at Carly's wedding."

"Good point. No matter, I can always toast Nicole's farewell another night." Because he had a feeling that the jagged pain that had taken up residence in his chest when she left would be there for many, many nights to come.

BY ALL RIGHTS, Nicole should be sick as a dog this morning. She'd barely eaten her food at last night's rehearsal dinner, she hadn't slept well in three days and she'd sobbed through half the night. But her stomach, if not her spirit, was completely serene. It's as if the babies sensed that she was already stretched to her wit's end and had decided to take it easy on her today.

Still, even though she felt all right physically, her emotions must be clear on her face because Adele's eyes were full of concern.

"I hate leaving you," Adele said, sitting on the foot of the couch where Nicole was tucked around a pillow. "If it weren't my daughter's wedding..."

"Of course you should go!" Nicole attempted a teasing smile. "After all the work I did to introduce you back into their lives, I'd be furious if you missed this. With any luck, Carly will be too smitten with the groom to notice my absence, but maybe sometime later, you can mention that I was feeling really sick today." Heartsick was a kind of sick, wasn't it?

"I know I already asked this last night, but are you sure you don't want to tell me what happened?"

"There's not much to tell." Except that the guy she'd been falling in love with suddenly claimed to feel the same way about her. Odd how that felt like a tragedy and not something to celebrate. "I decided that, in light of how emotional I've been lately, it was better to go ahead and say goodbye to Daniel instead of drawing it out. You know how they say everyone cries at weddings? I was afraid that if I started, I wouldn't be able to stop."

Adele heaved a sigh. "But telling him goodbye hurt more than you thought it would."

"I know, you tried to warn me." The prediction had been that it would end with Nicole in her pajamas, eating ice cream and listening to sad music. Well, she hadn't resorted to frozen dairy or power ballads yet. But she *was* curled up on the sofa in flannel jammies.

"Oh, honey. I'm not trying to say I told you so. It's just that I know what an openhearted person you are. You said you and Daniel were having fun but that you wouldn't let yourself care. Caring about others is who you are! It's what's made you the best friend I've ever had. And it's how I know you'll make a terrific mom."

Sniffling, Nicole squeezed her hand. "Thank you. But you should really get going." She suppressed, just barely, the urge to ask Adele to bring ice cream back with her when she returned.

IT WAS A beautiful wedding. In the moments when Daniel could banish Nicole from his mind—which, admittedly, weren't many—he found himself smiling at the outpouring of love around him. So many friends and family crammed into the sanctuary to wish Carly and Luke well. Rosie's favorite battered elephant had even been made a special dress and had a place of honor in one of the front pews as Rosie's daddy and new mommy exchanged their vows.

The sweet scent of flowers filled the chapel, and the dark green and gold color scheme was seasonal without making the wedding look like Christmas redux. Before Daniel knew it, the ceremony was over. Funny, that a ritual meant to bond people together for the rest of eternity could be completed in under an hour. As soon as the photographer finished getting the last of the church photos, it would be time to return to the ranch, where caterers had been setting up all morning, for the reception.

Daniel had joked recently about seeing Nicole do the Chicken Dance at the reception. Now he just wanted to see her, period. Even though he'd known she wasn't coming, right up until the time they'd closed the doors after the bride's entrance, he'd kept a hopeful eye on the back of the sanctuary. Which had been foolish of him. Nicole Bennett was a woman who knew her mind. She'd risen at a comparatively young age to vice president because of her determination, and when she'd decided she wanted to have kids, by golly, she'd gone right out and made that happen, too. So if she said she didn't want to see Daniel again…

"Daniel!" At the front of the church, Carly had her hands on her hips, looking gorgeous but imperious in her wedding gown. "What are you waiting for? When the photographer said the bride's brothers and sisters, he meant you, too!"

"Right. Sorry." He didn't bother explaining that his mind had wandered. He simply made his way up to the altar, where everyone else was waiting. It didn't escape his notice that Lizzie was watching him with the same sympathetic worry Jacob had been showing all day.

As soon as the pictures were done, Lizzie touched the sleeve of his tuxedo jacket. "I couldn't help notice Mom came alone today," she whispered. "No Nicole?"

"No." He swallowed hard. "No Nicole."

After that, everyone was dismissed. People paired off around him to return to their cars—Savannah and Travis, Jet and Jasmine, Lizzie and Chris, Jacob and Mariana and today's newlyweds. Daniel was the only one who stood alone. But he didn't feel as separate from the rest as he had a few weeks ago. Then, he hadn't understood the wedding fever that seemed to be burning through his family. Now, even though Nicole wasn't interested in pursuing a relationship with him, at least he *got* it. He understood what the others had found and why they treasured it. He was happy for them in a way that hadn't been possible before.

And he'd miss them all when he moved to Colorado. With Nicole rejecting his offer that they build a real relationship, turning down the job to be close to her was pointless. He'd explained his decision that morning to Jacob, who'd accepted it with a solemn nod, but today wasn't the right time to share the news with everyone else.

To accommodate the crowd invited to the reception at the ranch, valets had been hired. Daniel handed over the keys to his pickup, seeing the Roughneck with new eyes. It was a place of celebration today, bedecked in flowers and bows, a bandstand and a portable dance floor beneath a huge tent that also accommodated tables and chairs and space heaters. He politely refused the glass of champagne a waiter offered. If he started drinking, he might get maudlin and focus on his own unhappiness instead of Carly's joy. Of course, that was probably going to happen anyway, but why accelerate the process? His sister deserved wall-to-wall smiles today.

"How are you doing?"

He turned to find Savannah smiling gently at him. Sighing, he shook his head ruefully. "Does *everyone* know that I'm pining over Nicole?"

"Well…it was hard to miss the way you were all lit up at Christmas, when she was next to you. You glowed brighter than the lights on the tree. Now she's not here. And you're decidedly unglowy. Hang in there."

"Is this where you tell me there are other fish in the sea?" He appreciated the effort, but he didn't think platitudes were going to help.

She frowned. "No, I don't think so. Have you considered that maybe the answer is trying harder to catch the fish you want?" With that, she left him to go speak to the cousin waving from across the tent.

He was bemused by her advice. It wasn't as if he'd

let Nicole slip through his fingers without telling her how he felt. Savannah was definitely not the only one who'd noticed the quiet misery he was trying to mask. While Jasmine danced ring-around-the-rosy style with her giggling twin girls, Jet came up to Daniel and offered him a beer.

"Thanks." Daniel sat it on the table in front of him. "Surprised you're not out there dancing with them."

"Nah. Jasmine's girls have taken to me better than I had any right to expect, but they still need some mommy-daughter time. Besides, I wanted to catch you. I...know you've always felt more comfortable talking to Jacob. Why wouldn't you? He's older and definitely wiser. I know people have trouble taking me seriously."

That might have been true, once, but no one who'd seen Jet's devotion to his fiancée could question how serious he was about her and her girls. Daniel envied him the opportunity. How could he demonstrate to Nicole that he wanted to be there for her *and* the babies when they weren't even born yet?

"Anyway," Jet continued, "I just wanted to let you know that I'm here, too. If you ever need to talk brother to brother."

Not, Daniel noticed, stepbrother to stepbrother. Although he'd made the distinction all these years, it seemed that the Barons did not. No, they'd rallied around him when he'd been injured, insisting on driving him to his medical appointments, teasing him about Nicole and all finding opportunities at Christmas to tell him how wonderful she was. Growing up, he'd resented the Barons for not letting him in. But maybe he hadn't given them enough opportunity to include him.

"Thank you," Daniel said, genuinely touched by Jet's concern. "I appreciate the offer."

"We should get together more. Shoot pool or throw darts now that your shoulder is healing."

"I… Actually, I won't be in town much longer."

Jet grinned. "You're going to San Antonio, aren't you? Awesome. I just won ten bucks."

"No! I'm going to Colorado." His siblings were betting on him? Some of his newly discovered warm feelings chilled slightly. "I've been offered a job on a ranch there."

"But Nicole isn't in Colorado." Jet said the words with exaggerated patience.

"Coincidentally, Nicole doesn't want to see me again."

"Then she's crazy. You two are great together."

"Were," Daniel corrected. "We *were* great together." But now she was moving forward with her life. Colorado was his opportunity to do the same.

"Um…maybe we should take five." Sierra Bailey handed Daniel his towel, her hazel eyes wide with concern. "And you know it's bad when I say that because I'm hard-core."

He almost managed a smile for the physical therapist. "You want people to believe that, but I'm starting to think you're a softie inside."

She snorted. "I thought you ended up in the hospital for a shoulder wound, not a head injury." She waited while he took a slug from his bottle of water. "Now, you want to tell me why you seem hell-bent on kicking an invisible person's ass today?"

It was his own ass he wanted to kick. He'd waited too long. The morning after the wedding, he'd tried Nicole's cell. He'd left her a few messages and even tried calling her at work, where the perky receptionist maintained that she was unavailable. Not wanting to be a stalker, he hadn't shown up at her apartment or place of business. Until yesterday morning. He'd been desperate enough to go by the apartment.

Adele had let him in, and he could see that she was in the midst of packing. She'd informed him in grave tones that Nicole had caught a flight to San Antonio the previous night. *And, Daniel, she doesn't want to hear from you.*

Even though he'd told Jet and Jacob that it was over with Nicole, that he'd accepted it, apparently he hadn't believed until that moment Nicole would leave without saying goodbye. *She said her goodbyes. At the rehearsal dinner, remember?*

"Yo." Sierra snapped her fingers in front of his face. "I was just kidding about the head injury, but now you have me worried. That bull you fell off didn't kick you in the noggin, did it? How often do you zone out like this?"

"Sorry, guess you were right about my overdoing it today. Didn't mean to be so intense, just trying to get the most out of our last session." Tomorrow afternoon, he was booked on a flight to Denver. He was going to crash with Bodie and look for a place near the Double F. Then he'd come back some weekend in late January or February, pack the rest of his stuff onto his truck and put his house up for sale.

"I know relocating can get hectic, but promise me

you'll find a good physical therapist right away," Sierra said. "I've put a lot of work into you, and I don't want my effort going to waste."

"I promise."

She nodded, appeased. "If you keep up with the kind of determination you've been showing, you'll be your old self again in no time."

Much as he wanted to believe her assurance, he couldn't. Losing Nicole hurt a hell of a lot more than being thrown from a bull. Even with the miles he planned to put between them and the conventional wisdom that time healed all wounds, Daniel doubted he'd ever be the same again.

AN AUTOMATED VOICE through overhead speakers repeated the message about liquids in carry-on luggage. It was the third time Daniel had heard it since getting into the security line. Ahead of him, a group of teenagers were enthusiastically discussing skiing. Behind him, a couple was arguing about which one of them was supposed to have booked the rental car they were going to need when they reached Denver.

How pathetic was it that Daniel envied their bickering? He and Nicole would never have any of those silly, day-to-day disagreements. They also wouldn't have the opportunity to make up afterward. They wouldn't share nicknames or closet space or inside jokes. And he suddenly realized he wanted all of those things.

Saying goodbye to his siblings this morning had been more emotional than he could have guessed a month ago. Carly hadn't been there, but she'd sent him a text wishing him luck from her honeymoon hotel.

Much as he might miss his brothers and sisters, he thought it was better for his self-preservation not to be surrounded by a quintet of happily married couples. Hopefully, by the time he returned for Jacob and Mariana's wedding in the spring, he—

"Daniel!"

Weird. There were probably a dozen Daniels in the airport—it wasn't an uncommon name—but the person shouting actually *sounded* like Jacob. Probably because Daniel had just been thinking about him.

"Daniel, get out of line. We need to talk to you!"

Wait, that actually was Jacob. Daniel cast a startled glance behind him. What the hell? Jacob, Jet, Lizzie and Savannah were all motioning toward him.

Jet grinned. "We can use Dad's credit card to buy tickets to Denver and talk to you there, but it would be a lot easier if you just heard us out now."

Whatever they had to say, they'd driven all this way. He might as well spare them a few minutes. Apologizing to the people he passed, he backtracked his way through line and exited the security area.

"Guys, we already said goodbye," he reminded them. "This morning."

"This isn't goodbye," Lizzie said. "This is an intervention. Individually, we weren't going to interfere. But then we started talking after you left and—"

"And we think you're being an idiot," Jet said cheerfully. "None of us have ever seen you as happy as you were with Nicole."

Daniel ground his teeth. "In case it's escaped your collective memory, *she* dumped *me*."

"Are you sure?" Jacob asked. "Because—"

"Of course I'm sure!" Every word of the awful conversation was carved into his memory. She'd likened him to her mother, the addict who'd made promises but never came back to collect her daughter.

"All I meant," Jacob clarified, "is that sometimes you have to try again, be willing not to give up even when the other person is. You remember how I screwed up with Mariana, right? It took some serious effort to fix things."

Lizzie nodded. "I love Chris with my heart and soul, but finding our path wasn't easy. There are lots of opportunities for detours. Maybe you and Nicole just took a wrong turn. It might not be too late. But if you get on that plane…"

Were his siblings right, or were they all just so in love that it was giving them a false sense of optimism? He thought again about what Nicole had said, about the mother who'd let her down and hadn't been willing to give her something permanent. How could he expect Nicole to trust his commitment to her when he'd booked a flight out of the state at the first real obstacle? Just because other people had been willing to write her off didn't mean he was.

"What am I doing here?" he wondered aloud. "I should be on my way to San Antonio."

"Hot damn!" Jet grinned at Savannah. "You owe me ten bucks."

"No, I don't. You said, 'Bet you ten bucks he goes after her.' I didn't actually take the bet."

"Here." Daniel pulled out his wallet and handed Jet a ten. "It's the least I owe you for stopping me from making the biggest mistake of my life." Overcome by a rush of gratitude, he smiled. "I owe you all."

Lizzie threw her arms around him, and the next thing he knew, he was being mobbed in a group hug.

Jacob met his eyes over their sister's head. "Don't mention it. That's what family is for."

THE KNOCK AT the door made Nicole want to sing the hallelujah chorus. Thank God for restaurants that delivered. She hadn't realized when she'd crawled beneath her sheets last night how bare the cupboards were. Obviously she hadn't left produce or other perishables in her house, but shouldn't she at least have a can of soup rolling around somewhere? Mental note: *get better at stocking up supplies before the babies come.*

With purse in hand and plans to tip extravagantly, she swung open the door. Which she then had to cling to in order to keep herself upright. "D-Daniel."

"May I come in?"

No. If she let him in, she might throw herself at him, and that could send mixed messages. "How do you even know where I live?"

"Christopher."

"Traitor," she muttered, averting her gaze. He looked good, dammit, his dark hair rumpled, his jeans fitting way too well for her peace of mind. Trying to sound resolved, and not like someone who had all the willpower of pudding, she said, "You shouldn't have come here."

"I disagree. I had something very important to tell you, and you wouldn't return my calls." He held up a hand when she started to speak. "I'm actually glad you didn't. Because what I need to say should really be shared in person, anyway. Nicole, I love you."

Her knees trembled. "You said that before. It doesn't—"

"When I told you that I loved you before, you said that my change of heart happened too fast for you to believe it. But here's the thing, you didn't so much *change* my heart as reach it. Maybe the only thing that's changed is that I've decided not to let fear stop me from going after what I want. It's like bull riding. They talk about how it's not a matter of 'if' someone gets hurt, it's a matter of 'when.' I did rodeo for years, knowing there was a strong likelihood of landing on my ass and getting busted up. But I still went for it."

He paused, then gave her a heart-melting smile. "You have more power to hurt me than any animal I was ever in the ring with, Nicole, but you're worth the risk."

Did she even want that power? She hadn't asked for responsibility over his heart; she had enough trouble managing her own. She bit her lip in a vain attempt to keep from crying. "Daniel, my situation is complicated. I appreciate what you're saying, but—"

He took her hands in his. "I know you're worried about what happens when the babies come. Truthfully, that makes me a little nervous, too. But I know I want to be here. I know I want to go through it with you and get to hold them and see how much they look like their mama. You should have seen the kids at the wedding. They really got to me, and it wasn't how cute they were in their lacy dresses or miniature tuxes. It was how much they love their parents and vice versa.

Jacob didn't ask for Cody to come into his life, but I can honestly say my brother's never been happier. I want that chance for happiness, too."

"You're making it really hard to say no," she told him. Could she and Daniel find lasting happiness together?

When he stroked her hair away from her face and glanced down, his intention of kissing her evident in his gaze, she didn't turn him away. She rose on tiptoe to meet him. His lips brushed hers in an almost reverent caress, but when she opened her mouth beneath his, he groaned and deepened their kiss, taking everything she had to offer and making her body sizzle with need.

Behind them, a throat cleared. "Ahem. Is this a, uh, bad time?"

Nicole glanced behind Daniel and found a perplexed delivery boy on the sidewalk staring at them. She laughed. "Bad? No." To Daniel, she said, "This is very, very good."

"Does this mean I can come in now?" he whispered. "If we stay on your front porch, we may end up breaking some public-decency laws."

She paid the delivery boy, then dragged Daniel inside. "You meant what you said out there?" she asked breathlessly.

"Every word of it."

She let him pull her into his strong arms, then snuggled against him, loving his heat and the familiar male scent of him. As a girl, she'd dreamed of one day having a home with someone who loved her enough to stay forever. Could she have been lucky enough to have found that with Daniel Baron? "I love you."

"I love you, too. But I know words aren't guarantees. Which is why I will spend every day proving it to you." He lowered his head, claiming her mouth in a fervent kiss. "Starting right now."

Epilogue

Compared with giving birth, holding on to a bucking bull for dear life was a stroll through the park. Daniel was amazed at his wife's strength as she brought their twins into the world. It had been difficult for the OB to get clear enough sonograms of each baby to determine the gender, so they hadn't known what to expect. Now Daniel found himself holding a beautiful newborn girl in his arms while her brother was being bundled into a blanket to hand to Nicole.

"You did it," he whispered to Nicole. "You are a miracle."

"Not a miracle. Just a very tired, very happy woman."

He kissed her on the forehead, careful not to smush their infant daughter between them. *I'm a father.* His heart expanded with pride and love and terror and joy. So much joy. The fear was there sometimes, the thought that he couldn't possibly be this lucky, that something might happen, but the love he felt for Nicole was stronger than anything else. Every day he loved her more and tried to find ways to keep his pledge about proving it to her.

The first feeding was a little tricky, but he held one

baby, then swapped with Nicole. He had a suspicion that, for the next few months, their lives would feel a little like a juggling act. But he'd already arranged time off at the farm outside San Antonio where they raised show horses. He planned to be by his wife's side so that they could get the hang of parenting together. And Lord knew they had plenty of people to call for advice.

On the day he'd married Nicole in a small outdoor ceremony, surrounded by bluebonnets, she'd teased that she'd always envied large families. "I never dreamed that I'd be in one *this* big." Ten brothers- and sisters-in-law.

"You'll get used to it," he'd promised her. Truthfully, she'd adapted much better than he had. He'd spent too many years feeling like an outsider instead of doing anything to rectify the situation. Luckily for him, Barons were a stubborn lot. His siblings never gave up on him.

Several members of the family had made the trip to San Antonio. Others had promised to visit once Nicole had been released from the hospital so that they could help at home. "When are visitors allowed to come say hello?" Daniel asked the nurse.

"You can bring some in now, but only a couple at a time."

They sent the nurse out to get Jacob and Adele. The older woman was grinning from ear to ear even as tears spilled down her cheeks.

"Make room for the honorary grandmama," she said.

"And one very proud uncle," Jacob added. "Cody

already asked when he could play with his new cousins. Mariana's explaining that it will take a while."

Jacob hugged his brother while a nurse handed Adele the baby girl. "She's beautiful," Adele said. "So tiny and perfect."

Daniel stood by his wife, who held their son. "They both are." His eyes burned. It was surreal that one man could be so blessed. The family members crowded into the hall in a show of love and support, meeting his two children for the first time, and, at the center of it all, the amazing woman who'd agreed to spend her life with him. Who'd have thought the happiest day of his life would take place in a hospital?

* * * * *

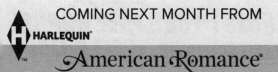

COMING NEXT MONTH FROM

HARLEQUIN®
American Romance®

Available December 2, 2014

#1525 LONE STAR CHRISTMAS
McCabe Multiples • by Cathy Gillen Thacker
Callie McCabe-Grimes's plan is to get through the holidays with her heart intact. Nash Echols, Christmas tree ranch owner, prefers celebrating Christmas to the max. But it's Callie's preschool son who shows them both the way Christmas should be celebrated!

#1526 A TEXAS HOLIDAY MIRACLE
by Linda Warren
When six-year-old Emma learns that Santa doesn't exist, Lacey Carroll does everything she can to convince the little girl that the Christmas spirit is alive and well...with a little help from seemingly Scrooge-like next-door neighbor Gabe Garrison.

#1527 CHRISTMAS COWBOY DUET
Forever, Texas • by Marie Ferrarella
Talent scout Whitney never expected to find the next big thing in country music in Forever, Texas. But can she convince the mischievous Liam to take a chance on the big stage...and on her?

#1528 CHRISTMAS WITH THE RANCHER
by Mary Leo
Real estate mogul Bella Biondi doesn't have time for the holidays—until her childhood sweetheart, Travis Granger, turns her structured world upside down with his easy cowboy charm and love for everything Christmas!

YOU CAN FIND MORE INFORMATION ON UPCOMING HARLEQUIN® TITLES, FREE EXCERPTS AND MORE AT WWW.HARLEQUIN.COM.

HARCNM1114

REQUEST YOUR FREE BOOKS!
2 FREE NOVELS PLUS 2 FREE GIFTS!

 HARLEQUIN®

LOVE, HOME & HAPPINESS

YES! Please send me 2 FREE Harlequin® American Romance® novels and my 2 FREE gifts (gifts are worth about $10). After receiving them, if I don't wish to receive any more books, I can return the shipping statement marked "cancel." If I don't cancel, I will receive 4 brand-new novels every month and be billed just $4.74 per book in the U.S. or $5.24 per book in Canada. That's a savings of at least 14% off the cover price! It's quite a bargain! Shipping and handling is just 50¢ per book in the U.S. and 75¢ per book in Canada.* I understand that accepting the 2 free books and gifts places me under no obligation to buy anything. I can always return a shipment and cancel at any time. Even if I never buy another book, the two free books and gifts are mine to keep forever.

154/354 HDN F4YN

Name	(PLEASE PRINT)	
Address		Apt. #
City	State/Prov.	Zip/Postal Code

Signature (if under 18, a parent or guardian must sign)

Mail to the **Harlequin® Reader Service:**
IN U.S.A.: P.O. Box 1867, Buffalo, NY 14240-1867
IN CANADA: P.O. Box 609, Fort Erie, Ontario L2A 5X3

Want to try two free books from another line?
Call 1-800-873-8635 or visit www.ReaderService.com.

* Terms and prices subject to change without notice. Prices do not include applicable taxes. Sales tax applicable in N.Y. Canadian residents will be charged applicable taxes. Offer not valid in Quebec. This offer is limited to one order per household. Not valid for current subscribers to Harlequin American Romance books. All orders subject to credit approval. Credit or debit balances in a customer's account(s) may be offset by any other outstanding balance owed by or to the customer. Please allow 4 to 6 weeks for delivery. Offer available while quantities last.

Your Privacy—The Harlequin® Reader Service is committed to protecting your privacy. Our Privacy Policy is available online at www.ReaderService.com or upon request from the Harlequin Reader Service.

We make a portion of our mailing list available to reputable third parties that offer products we believe may interest you. If you prefer that we not exchange your name with third parties, or if you wish to clarify or modify your communication preferences, please visit us at www.ReaderService.com/consumerschoice or write to us at Harlequin Reader Service Preference Service, P.O. Box 9062, Buffalo, NY 14269. Include your complete name and address.

HARI3R

Nash Echols dropped a fresh-cut Christmas tree onto the
bed of a flatbed truck. He watched as a luxuriously outfit-
ted red SUV tore through the late November gloom and
came to an abrupt stop on the old logging trail.

"Well, here comes trouble," he murmured, when the
driver door opened and two equally fancy peacock-blue
boots hit the running board.

His glance moved upward, taking in every elegant inch
of the cowgirl marching toward him. He guessed the sassy
spitfire to be in her early thirties, like him. She glared while
she moved, her hands clapped over her ears to shut out the
concurrent whine of a dozen power saws.

Nash lifted a leather-gloved hand.

One by one his crew stopped, until the Texas mountain-
side was eerily quiet, and only the smell of fresh-cut pine
hung in the air. And still the determined woman advanced,
chin-length dark brown curls framing her even lovelier face.

He eased off his hard hat and ear protectors.

Indignant color highlighting her delicately sculpted
cheeks, she stopped just short of him and propped her hands
on her slender denim-clad hips. "You're killing me, using
all those chain saws at once!" Her aqua-blue eyes narrowed.
"You know that, don't you?"

Actually, Nash hadn't.

Her chin lifted another notch. *"You have to stop!"*

At that, he couldn't help but laugh. It was one thing for this little lady to pay him an unannounced visit, another for her to try to shut him down. "Says who?" he challenged right back.

She angled her thumb at her sternum, unwittingly drawing his glance to her full, luscious breasts beneath the fitted red velvet Western shirt, visible beneath her open wool coat. "Says me!"

"And you are?"

"Callie McCabe-Grimes."

Of course she was from one of the most famous and powerful clans in the Lone Star State. He should have figured that out from the moment she'd barged onto his property.

Nash indicated the stacks of freshly cut Christmas trees around them, aware the last thing he needed in his life was another person not into celebrating the holidays. "Sure that's not Grinch?"

Look for LONE STAR CHRISTMAS
by Cathy Gillen Thacker from the
***McCABE MULTIPLES** miniseries from*
Harlequin American Romance.

Available December 2014
wherever books and ebooks are sold.

American Romance

A time for magic...and new beginnings?

Ever since he lost his son in an accident, Gabe has shut
out the world. But even in his peaceful hometown, his
privacy is invaded by the quirky, dynamic blonde
Lacey Carroll and her kid sister, who's already bonding
with his dog. And Lacey just enlisted him in a holiday
campaign regarding a certain red-suited reindeer driver.
Can her unique brand of healing magic make this a season
of second chances—for all of them?

Look for
A Texas Holiday Miracle
by LINDA WARREN

Available December 2014
wherever books and ebooks are sold.